2417

Running

CARA HOFFMAN

SIMON & SCHUSTER

New York   London   Toronto   Sydney   New Delhi

Simon & Schuster
1230 Avenue of the Americas
New York, NY 10020

First Simon & Schuster hardcover edition March 2017

SIMON & SCHUSTER and colophon are registered trademarks of Simon & Schuster, Inc.

For information about special discounts for bulk purchases, please contact Simon & Schuster Special Sales at 1-866-506-1949 or business@simonandschuster.com.

The Simon & Schuster Speakers Bureau can bring authors to your live event. For more information or to book an event, contact the Simon & Schuster Speakers Bureau at 1-866-248-3049 or visit our website at www.simonspeakers.com.

Manufactured in the United States of America

1 3 5 7 9 10 8 6 4 2

Library of Congress Cataloging-in-Publication Data

ISBN 978-1-4767-5757-5
ISBN 978-1-4767-5759-9 (ebook)

For J. N.

First there is the World. Then there is the Other World. . . . the world of the stoplight, the no-smoking signs, the rental world, the split-rail fencing shielding hundreds of miles of barren wilderness from the human step. A place where by virtue of having been born centuries late one is denied access to earth or space, choice or movement. The bought-up world; the owned world. The world of coded sounds: the world of language, the world of lies.

—DAVID WOJNAROWICZ, *Close to the Knives: A Memoir of Disintegration*

Running

J asper died a week before I returned to Athens, so I never
saw him again. They carried him out and down and he
died in England, or maybe on the plane. There were wit-
nesses in the lobby. There was a story in the newspaper. There
was, the drunk boy said without raising his eyes to meet
mine, proof.

Out on the street, a hot breeze moved the suffocating air
around and kicked up grit from the gutter. I stood for a time
by the door of the bar waiting to feel something, then walked
in the direction of Monastiraki.

When I met Jasper in the spring of 1988, I still had fifty
dollars, which was fifty dollars more than I had now. He
wore a faded black T-shirt and dark pin-striped cutoffs that
looked like they'd once been the trousers of a school uniform. His lank, oily blond hair was shaved in the back, hung
in his face, and he was sweating.

"I need to make some money right away," I told him.

Jasper nodded, lit a cigarette.

"There's quite a lot of ways to do that here," he said, his voice smooth and kind, his pale green eyes trained on my remaining possessions.

We recognized one another. I wasn't a tourist. He'd get nothing for bringing me back to the hotel.

We stood in the aisle, away from the seated passengers, with our arms hanging out the window, the bright hot sun burning down and a breeze born from the speed of the train blowing in upon our faces. Outside, terraced slopes of silver-leaved olive trees dotted the rocky yellow landscape, and piles of plastic bottles lay strewn by the edge of the track. He told me about a punk show he'd seen in London where a guy set his cock on fire using aerosol hairspray, and about a journal Alexander Pushkin kept that had been published after being banned for one hundred years.

"I've been rewriting the want ads in dactylic hexameter," he said.

"Why?"

"Because it's funny. Because it makes them more beautiful," he said. "Obviously." Jasper described the city planning of Athens and the ruin that was London and the prospects of getting work in the olive groves of Artimeda. I wasn't used to people talking so much.

"Where you from?" he asked.

"The States," I said.

"Originally," he said. "I mean where are you from originally?"

"The United States."

He shrugged as if I hadn't understood the question. "Athens is okay," Jasper said. "But you can't sleep out and you can't sleep in the underground. The idea is to get to the islands. You know, make enough money in the city or picking fruit somewhere. Or," he said, "by better, quicker means."

His breath had the sweet medicinal bite of licorice and a cool flammable underlay. His eyes were a calm marbled green; skin so tender it looked like he might not yet shave; dimples beside a pair of fine, full lips. Jasper's was the kind of elegant placid face you saw in old portraits. His posture straight, his shoulders wide. It was only after half an hour of standing beside him that I noticed his left arm was in a cast.

As we got closer to Athens, ragged, hungry-looking boys holding leaflets jostled onto the train, crowding the aisles, leaning on the arms of seats, talking to people about the islands or the Plaka or Mount Olympus. Saying they'd bring you to a nice place to stay; they'd take you to the ruins, to the port, to the bluest waters waiting just one more town away.

"None of it," Jasper said, his eyes gone flat and dark as we approached the station, "is true."

Back then I also had a small bag. Carried my last pack of Camels and a lighter, my passport, newly exchanged blue drachma notes with statues of gods printed on them. I had a pair of cutoffs, a T-shirt, a pencil, some soap. I had a wool sweater, ammonium nitrate, electrical tape. I was flush with riches even after a year of sleeping out in train stations, church doorways, and parks. I had good boot laces. I had fire.

Now I was sufficiently pared down to the essentials. The sweater was unnecessary; the extra T-shirt had become a towel.

I'd come back to Athens after three months away picking olives, wandering the streets in Istanbul, and living in a border village that was a tight, rocky knot of land claimed alternately by Syria, Lebanon, and Palestine. I'd come back against every rational instinct for self-preservation I'd ever known.

We had lived together, Jasper and Milo, and me at a four-dollar-a-night hotel on Diligianni Street across from Larissis train station and a sick sliver of scrub grass littered with condoms and empty bottles that people called a park. Sometimes when Declan was between jobs he would stay there too.

The city was like a beacon. And it drew us from wherever we'd been left. For me, the outskirts of a smoke jumpers' base in a cold mountain town, for Jasper and Milo the London suburbs and rain-soaked council housing of Manchester. We were looking for nothing and had found it in Athens: Demeter's lips white as stone, Apollo's yellow mantle sun washed, sanded, windblown to granite. The barren, blighted street outside our room in the low white ruin of the red-light district smelled like burning oil and a sooty haze hung in the middle distance. The hotel had no sign, but everyone called it Olympos.

Running

I first arrived in Greece by boat the year before, and didn't have money for meals. I had been hungry on that trip from Brindisi in a way I'd never experienced before. The heat, the vast, wind-filled open ocean, dark water shining like mercury beneath the sun; bright blue sky and wind, salt and sweat drying against your skin. I'd had a deck-class ticket and drifted along near the dining room's outdoor tables waiting for people to leave before they finished their meals. Then I'd slip in quickly for their leftovers. People think they need things. Money or respect or clean sheets. But they don't. You can wash your hair and brush your teeth with hand soap. You can sleep outside. You can eat whatever's there.

Once you're in a warm place, you can live for years and years and years on one five-dollar bill to the next. Five dollars is a reasonable amount of money to come across in the course of a day.

Jasper and Milo knew this before I did; good at surviving week to week, sipping sweetly from bottles of ouzo and Metaxa, reeling arm in arm before the Parthenon or the big television at Drinks Time. They were runners. We were all runners.

I tried to imagine it now, to feel their presence again amid the concrete and noise, to hear Jasper's footsteps on the slick granite sidewalk. There was no money left to buy a train ticket or a deck-class. I'd been robbed in Tarlabasi and the last of the money we had made together was gone. I could stay or hitchhike but I was weighted down, tied, tired.

The dementing arid heat of day was high and powerful

and I could feel the sweat crawling across my scalp. Compact cars sped by on the dirty thoroughfare. I turned up Karolou Street and walked on the shadowed side along a block of empty buildings and shuttered cafés to get some reprieve from the sun's glare and the roar of the highway.

I stopped at a kiosk to ask for a cup of water and when the man inside handed it to me his fingers grazed mine for a second and I had to look away.

Milo Rollock left school in the spring of 1987 because he believed he could make money fighting. He had been living with his mother in a council estate in Manchester when Jasper came out of nowhere. Walked down the church basement steps two rounds in, wearing a wet, rumpled Eton uniform. He was pissed, reckless; hovering on the outskirts of some eclipsed nihility to see if he could get himself stomped, and there were always people to oblige a boy like that.

Milo bit down on his mouth guard. This boy was like an apparition. He'd shown up so that people would know. Not suspect but *know*. He'd shown up to force Milo's hand.

Milo's mother worked assembly line until made redundant. They were home all day. Beans on toast for two meals and tea. She'd tried not to let him out of the building when he was a boy except for school. Saw something in him that needed protecting; all but made the whole of Salford promise to watch out for him. She was powerful, Colleen, powerful in the building and in the neighborhood. He never knew why.

There was nothing outside Canon Green Court but a square metal playground on a cracked cement slope where junkies nodded out on benches and kids splashed in puddles or played rough. Football games in the court were so violent, boys would sometimes search for teeth that'd scattered like dice cross the pavement.

Colleen was twenty-seven when Milo was in junior school, wore her hair in long braids that smelled of coconut oil; stayed up reading and smoking all night, listening to the 13th Floor Elevators on a little Bakelite record player she'd had since she was a girl. He'd curl up beside her sometimes and they'd paint their toenails or talk about books, build tiny houses out of paper, and set them alight in the ashtray.

From his room Milo could see the rooftops of the city, low slate-shingled row houses and stout chimneys, and in the distance the metal roofs of the warehouses and the factory stacks pumping out opaque plumes of orange and gunmetal gray in a long rushing column that cut through the rain. You could smell the smoke with the windows open and sometimes with the windows shut; sulfur, rubber. It burned your eyes.

During the day, streets were jammed with people going about working. But it was a ghost town after dark, the towers and stacks almost invisible against the sooty evening sky. He would gaze out upon these columns and dream about being down in the empty cobbled streets, small among the tall, wide weight of buildings, cradled by the whole filthy town, running wild. He wanted to go kick the ball around, but even that scared Colleen, seemed to scare her more the older he got. So he stayed home and read Jean Genet, because she said *Our Lady of the Flowers* had been written twice, once destroyed by prison guards. She said it was good. And she was right. She was educated, Colleen.

When he started disobeying, fighting, not coming right up after school, she saw to it that he box. Just like that: brought him to the gym, dropped him off. The men there knew her name and for some reason they knew his, treated him like he was dead tough even though they could already tell. Everyone could. She did right by bringing him there.

Jasper'd said that night, down in the basement, that he'd left school and hitched north that morning; that he'd stopped at every bar between Windsor and Salford; that he'd heard the bell for the rounds outside while he was pissing by the cellar door, and had a premonition, which was why he'd bet on Milo. And now wanted to buy him a round. All these claims seemed utter shite. Sixteen, not a hair on his face, blond and pale, his wrists jutting out of a shaggy wool jacket that smelled like wet dog and sported the fancy crest: a lion, white flowers on a black field. His weight slung low in his hips, the delicate way he held his cigarette, that boy was not coming close to passing. Didn't *care* about passing; stared around the place like it might have been an amusing hallucination. Milo got him out of there because he was embarrassed, because he was crushed by his beauty, because he knew Jasper's blood would make a mess of the floor.

Their shoulders brushed against one another's as they walked and Milo cut his eyes away until they were out and on the street and even then he knew the boy would get him in trouble. The roads were slick and shining beneath the streetlamps and they trudged, hunched against the chill, hands in pockets through the misting drizzle from pub to pub, looking past one another, sitting close behind their drinks. Jasper's finger lightly grazing the back of Milo's dark, swollen-knuckled hand was already more than he'd thought possible in this world.

Out on the docks past midnight with the black water lapping against the break wall, Milo pressed his body against Jasper's and felt the boy's breath on his lips, put his hand up beneath Jasper's oxford to feel his thin smooth chest, brought his face down against his skin. His nipples were hard, petal pink, tasting of sweat. When Jasper knelt before him glassy-eyed, smiling, he felt his skin grow tighter. Tight to bursting at his touch, at his wet mouth, his tongue, the slick hard edge of his teeth. Jasper's throat opened as Milo moved deeper, holding fistfuls of his rain-soaked white-blond hair.

Milo left with him that night. They were on a ferry to Calais next morning still drunk. As the ship left dock, Jasper pulled a square of glossy paper from his jacket pocket and unfolded it: a map of the continents torn from an encyclopedia.

"The problem is," he'd said, and Milo could still taste him, didn't care if anyone saw how close they stood, "there's no way out."

A runner's job is to lie about where he lives, then convince people to come home with him. Every runner's hotel was nearly identical, part of a cluster of brick and concrete walk-ups in the red-light district; none had bathrooms in the room, rarely was there hot water, never was there breakfast. They were stifling, blazing hot in summer, and far away from the kind of ruins everyone wanted to see.

We would take the train outside the city to a smaller city—Elefsina or Corinth—and then get the next train back in, which would be packed with tourists from Northern Europe or the port at Brindisi.

Our job was to intercept them, sell them on our hotel while they were still captive on the train, dreaming about the birthplace of civilization. Then we'd walk them from the station to Olympos and make sure they checked in. Ideally two or more people ran a train. One laughed at the other's jokes, one confirmed the other's lies. And, back at Olympos, one stood behind the tourists so they didn't leave once they saw what the hotel was really like. After they had checked in and paid, after their passports were taken and stored, we got our commission money and went directly to Drinks Time to spend it. What happened later to all their nice things was purely a matter of chance.

In exchange for these services, we lived for free in a small room on the top floor where we could see, at night and far in the distance, the tiny Acropolis lit up in the twilight haze like a state park diorama.

Apart from our room and one other, the top floor was gone, the walls had crumbled; brick and plaster and cinder blocks lay strewn across the cracked tile and you could see beyond the missing wall what had once been a rooftop terrace. It was the kind of mess caused by a construction project given up mid way. Or, if you are more observant, by a small bomb.

Declan was not truly a runner. Sometimes he went away to places where there were wars and came back with money. Boyhood skills he'd honed fighting the Royal Ulster Constabulary made for a good second career when he had to leave Ireland. Now he lived in hotels. In Athens for years, and, before that, Gaza, Angola.

We were supposed to think of ourselves as a squad, Declan said, to strategize our runs, to answer to him and "be good," never draw attention to ourselves. We were like the Spartans, he said. Spartan soldiers.

"Too right," Jasper said. "But not for the reasons he thinks."

The names Seamus, Joseph, and Tommy were tattooed on Declan's right forearm. A rising phoenix bloomed in faded red across his muscled back, interlocking shamrocks on the side of his neck, his arms a junkyard of symbols, his earlobes marked with stars. He saw the three of us as some kind of project: a girl and two queers, people in need of protection, people who'd be grateful to him, because without him, he reasoned, we'd be dead. We were the way he tithed.

Declan was paranoid about police and extradition. He'd mention having to kill one of us at least once a day, wanted our obedience, insisted on politeness; mind your fucking manners and watch your fucking mouth. I liked his sense of humor but never understood why he couldn't keep quiet about what he did.

"'Cause he's a fucking nutter," Jasper said. "Really not a mystery, is it? Man who stabs a cat, throws it from the balcony on passersby—isn't exactly inauspicious, now, is he?"

"When did he do that?" I asked.

"He didn't," Milo said.

"He might have," Jasper said. "We don't know. We're not with him every second of the day."

Standing in line at a kiosk outside Larissis station in the morning amid the crush of people pressing past, clean and bright for work in the dirty city, some wearing dust masks against the smog, we lined up to buy our cigarettes and beer and lemon crème cookies, staples for the ride and the run. We were tired but feeling good in the relative cool and didn't mind when an English tourist carrying a tall pack cut in front of us.

Declan did mind, though; tapped the man on the shoulder, asked him to step aside. The man's eyes skated over us, rested for a second too long on Milo, before he smirked and spat on the sidewalk. Milo winced and Jasper started laughing and Declan grabbed the man rough and quick by the sides of his face, pulled him forward with a vicious nod, snapping the man's nose flat. He yelped, twisted away; blood poured down his shirt, painted Declan's forehead bright, splattered across the sidewalk.

People in line took no time at all to recognize what wasn't their business.

"You'll have to get that set," Declan said, rubbing his head, then licking the man's blood from his fingers.

"You'll have to get that set," we said for weeks after.

No one was unhappy when Declan decided to find a more respectable hotel to live in. He said the highway noise on Diligianni was ruining his beauty sleep. Plus it was always a good idea to move around, just in case.

"Don't get any ideas," he told us. "I could always kill youse now to have peace of mind. But dumping three bodies is not a thing I'm bound to undertake at the present moment. Y'can thank me."

Jasper raised his bottle to that. I looked up from my book and nodded. Milo said "Thank you" and stood to help him pack.

The last place I'd seen Declan was Athens Inn. I was hoping he would still be there, sitting with Milo down in the vine-

covered courtyard, sipping ouzo and passing the time between trains.

The granite sidewalk was worn and slick, looked like
melting ice, and the neighborhood seemed older and more
lively. I hurried along, thinking of Milo's face, of how he must
be feeling if things the boy at DrinksTime told me were true.
A sudden shock of loneliness flooded my body and I couldn't
walk. I stood, refusing a sob that must have started in Milo's
chest and now somehow burned in mine. It was a mistake to
have left the bar one round behind.

In the lobby of Athens Inn, Declan was drinking water,
sitting alone at a café table. His face beaten elegant; high,
uneven cheekbones, flattened nose. His body, even in repose,
was a warning, built by fast and brutal acts.

A Greek soap opera played on a television atop the reception desk, and a dull gray ceiling fan whirred and clicked but
brought no relief. Declan was wearing a jean jacket despite
the heat and a pair of army boots like mine.

He'd no doubt seen me but waited until I was sitting
across from him to shut his book. A smile revealed the chip
in his left incisor, then he leaned in to kiss me, held my hand.

"To what do I owe this lovely surprise?" he asked, then
looked into my eyes to see if I knew about Jasper, nodded.
"Let's get some air," he said.

Out in the vicious glittering sun we sat on the steps surrounded by the bleak white buildings of the neighborhood,
their striped and slanted awnings pulled down against the
glare and heat and emptiness of day.

He put his hair back in a ponytail, revealing a black tattoo star.

"Who told you?" he asked.

"About five different cocksuckers sitting around Drinks Time," I said. "Stopped over when I got in, thinking he might be there." I pulled out a cigarette and lit it and he took it from my lips, threw it into the street.

"Milo been by to see you?" I asked.

"Y'know, it's puzzling," Declan said. "I've not seen Milo for days. And he didn't say good-bye. No farewell a tall. Last time someone left so rudely, she didn't turn up until"—he looked at his watch—"eight minutes ago."

"He say where he was headed?"

Declan smirked. "Nah. Figgered he'd gone to meet you, didn't I? Figgered the two of youse had a neat little plan."

"My only plan's to keep sleeping indoors; you know how it is."

"I don't," he said, and whatever he said next I was constitutionally incapable of hearing. I shaded my eyes and gazed across the street to where a man in a faded polo shirt and soccer sandals was trying to start his moped. Another man leaned over an upstairs balcony that was thick with climbing vines and potted flowers, and threw something metal that clanged against the curb. Declan was still talking, so I looked up and tested how long I could stare into the sun without blinking.

Declan believed in things only ruined people could: borders and nations and pride; family and loyalty; retribution.

He was everything Jasper and Milo and I had left behind; a cipher from the straight world spouting the gospel that had wrecked his own life. I could tell by his tone there was a summation coming, so I made myself pay attention to specific words.

"Some people just don't know how to stick together," he said. "But it could be worse. Some people don't know how to survive at all. Like your li'l mate Murat Christensen, am I right? You're not asking me about him, though, are you? You're not asking where *he* is."

I shut my eyes and flicked the lighter inside my pocket. I wanted another drink badly. Sweat was running down my back. A woman wearing a veil and a long burgundy dress walked by holding a pudgy baby with dark eyes. Few people passed at this hour in the afternoon. The heat was stupefying and there was no breeze, no noise, no motion at all.

Declan turned toward me and held my face, gently brushed the hair out of my eyes.

"When did you last eat?" he asked.

That day we'd met on the train, Jasper brought me back to Drinks Time and we sat in a haze of cigarette smoke which hung head level above the sticky wooden tables. The TV over the bar was blaring an American movie dubbed into Greek. A strong smell of bleach and beer and sour licorice permeated the place. People I'd seen on the train, runners, sat at tables near the front window, ragged and tan, jackal jawed, tipping back in their chairs, holding pints.

Three meticulously groomed middle-aged men and a younger, thinner man wearing a green silk shirt unbuttoned to the chest played dominoes and drank from little white cups at the back of the bar. Jasper watched them. When the younger man looked up, he smiled with a calculated shyness I could feel in my gut. Jasper held the man's gaze as he sipped the head of his pint, then looked away.

"They're always so nicely dressed," Jasper said. His strong delicate hands drummed beside his glass, nails bit short. He was thin, not grown into his skin; a regal jutting of wrist bones, collarbones. Dimples making what might have been a gaunt face childlike.

"I like these lads," he said. "I do. They have quite a lot of visitors here in the afternoon. I wonder where they eat supper. I'd like to go where they go." He finished his pint and put it on the table. "I'm so glad you're here," he went on. "Do you know how to drive? We should get a car. I'd like to drive, but it gets in the way of . . ." He gestured vaguely around. "Too hard to concentrate on it. Have you been to the Temple of Hephaestus?"

"I just got here half an hour ago," I told him.

"Right," he said. "Well. People are in awe of these things, you know. In absolute awe. But it's the damage they love, really; they *say* it's the history, but it's the *damage*. No one would care in the least if these things were new—covered with gaudy, bright primary colors like it was back then. They love the ruin and they love the cocks. I mean, how many penises can you *look* at? Honestly, how many?"

"Is there a limit?"

"Like, every last painting or sculpture of these *mythical* beings has someone with a hard-on, riding a horse with a hard-on, or fighting a centaur with a hard-on. Or roving through the countryside with some goat-footed satyr who's got a cock as big as your arm. You get—I'm quite serious, now; please try to hold it together, because I'm serious, I'm *not* joking—you get *penis* fatigue looking at these things. You ever see those herms?"

I shook my head.

"You know what I'm talking about? It's just a rectangular block of granite with a guy's head on top and—no other features, nothing—and then his johnson about halfway down. That's it. Head and cock. Nothing more. Bloody hilarious. Like the whole thing was dreamt up by ten-year-old boys. I saw this plate in the museum—you know, simple domestic plate; like, a *plate*, from which to eat *food*—and on it there's a soldier with an erection carrying a rabbit by the ears. The rabbit has an erection. It's sort of gloriously appalling." He sipped his beer, lit another cigarette with one he'd just finished.

The collar of Jasper's T-shirt was torn at the seam and dark marks like the shadows of fingers were visible beneath. I played with my lighter while I watched him exhale a cloud of smoke, his tongue resting at the edge of his teeth. The beer was fixing my hunger but I would need a real meal soon. Jasper's voice was smooth—each sentence held the edge of a joke or playful astonishment.

"It's nice the way you speak," I said, sipping from my pint.

"Can't be helped," he said. "I went to Eton."

"Where's that?" I asked. "I've never been."

We watched the rippling heat outside the window while cultivating a languid thrumming numbness. The boys by the window were louder now, except for one who had fallen asleep, his hand cradling his glass. The men in their nice clothes snapped dominoes against the table, clinked cups back onto their saucers. It wasn't until we stood that the whole room reeled.

Jasper put his hand on my shoulder to steady one of us and we walked back into the oven of the streets, moving fast to keep upright. Hot air rushed into my lungs and I squinted along beside him in the blinding light. Figures at the dark periphery of buildings made themselves out, two middle-aged men in tight button-down shirts open wide at the neck; they exchanged glances as we passed, their gaze sliding over us, calculating. The narrow streets curved one into another, a tangle of nameless places. Bare bulbs hung outside buildings above empty folding chairs, as if an interrogation were soon to take place. The flat slap of our shoes on pavement echoed as we walked past the smoke- and soot-stained remains of a building that had recently burned, and we emerged onto the wide, loud thoroughfare of Diligianni Street.

Olympos was like an architectural ghost, something that had once been regal and was now only missing police tape or plywood over the windows and door. "Home sweet home," Jasper said. We stood on the corner burst out laughing beneath the building's molting façade, doubled over, wiping tears from our cheeks, but really I was very glad to have arrived, and relieved to have a place to stay.

In the lobby an old man in horn-rimmed glasses sat eating an ear of roasted corn. We slipped past him and up the spiral stairs.

Inside Jasper's room, on a low metal-framed bed, a shirtless boy leaned against the wall reading. His skin was brown and his eyes were a dark, metallic hazel. He was using a pile of books as a bedside coffee table, and there was another pile spilled out across the floor in the center of the room. After sleeping outside on benches or inside on floors with crowds milling about, the place felt enormous and private and extravagant.

"You're a wee bit late, yeah?" the boy said. "Thought maybe it was some shite with drivers."

Jasper shook his head, leaned down, and kissed him on the mouth, then walked briskly past and opened the balcony door, kicked some bottles over to the side, and tossed my pack against the rail.

"Right, my love," Jasper said, exhaling a cloud of blue gray smoke and gesturing with his cast. "This is where you'll be staying. You must behave yourself or you'll upset my brother Milo. You may have heard of Milo Rollock. He's won several awards for hitting other men hard in the face at a small but exclusive gymnasium in Manchester. That's a place in England, Bridey. Manchester, England, it's called."

Milo unscrewed the cap on a bottle of ouzo, handed it to me, and I drank a few sips. I'd now spent every minute of the afternoon drinking a few sips. Jasper took the bottle next and poured the thin, translucent spirit down his throat.

Jasper said, "He's a poet as well, obviously. Just look at the man . . ."

Milo gave us a close-lipped smile, held out his hand. He had strong shoulders, had calm eyes. "Milo Rollock," he said formally, as if Jasper and I weren't staggering. A copy of the *Athens Times* was spread out in front of him, a pencil tucked behind his ear. I tried to see what books were on the stack by the bed, but looking down made the room spin.

"Bridey," I said taking his hand. He reached beneath the bed and pulled up a bottle of Amstel, uncapped it with a lighter, and handed it to me, then made room for me beside him. Patted the bed. I sat and drank.

"Where've y'come from?" Milo's accent was so thick, it sounded like he was speaking half in another language or had a speech impediment.

"The States," I said, sitting down. "By way of some other places."

Jasper appeared to be falling asleep standing up.

"Com'ed, handsome," Milo said to him. "Better sit down."

"I'll sit down, then," Jasper said. He reclined on the floor in front of us, leaned his head back against the bed, and Milo ran his hands through his hair, brushed the sweat from his forehead. I tipped the bottle of Amstel to Jasper's lips so he could drink. He shut his eyes and it was as if I could suddenly see him. I looked at his beautiful throat, the line of his lips, the bones in his jaw, the lovely hollow of his cheeks. His ribs were visible beneath his T-shirt. He had the palest skin, like something that had lived a life submerged. I wanted to put my mouth on his. I wanted to put my mouth all over him.

Milo watched me. Smiled, then turned to light a cigarette. "Must be tired from bein' with this joker all afternoon, yeah?"

"It was no trouble," I said.

"Evenin's lovely here once the temperature drops. He

won't be sober till morning." He casually pointed his chin at Jasper, who'd slumped down and was now lying flat on the floor. "But we'll go out for a wander, yeah? Go walk up round Monastiraki Square. Get you something to eat. You look hungry. Good ta get out. See the lights shinin' on the Acropolis in the dark."

"What're you reading?" I asked Milo.

"This? Just looking in the adverts for a better place for meself and this charmer. Tryna find a house-sit, yeah? On the islands, with any luck. And this"—he said, holding up a small hardback with a red cover—"is some poetry. You fancy it? Jasper got sent *The Holy Sonnets*, in a package."

A white moth fluttered around the lamp and then over Jasper's face. He reached up and caught it, put it quickly in his mouth, one white wing protruding from his lips, still fluttering, struggling, until he spit it out, dead and wet against his chest.

Milo laughed tensely through his teeth, brushed the moth to the floor, then took a long sip from the bottle and handed it to me. I drank and stretched out next to him.

"Listen to this," he said, turning a page of the book. "You'll like this."

We lived that way for months. The past was a physical feeling that sometimes washed over me; an unrealized ache in my bones, like after sleeping on hard floors, or drifting for weeks with little to eat. It was not a series of images, or memories; it was nothing that could be spoken.

Milo's story was as silent as mine but present on his face: a wide, flat nose, a strange ear, compassionate eyes filled with the abiding patience of one who has gotten by on little and tolerated much.

Jasper talked for all of us, in a fascinating and repulsive monologue I had first thought was a joke: Jasper playing piano for gatherings his parents had; going to the West End with his mother to the bakery he loved, to the club with his father during breaks from school; horse riding and punting and cricket. Summer by the sea. Christmases with thirty-foot trees. His father reading Dylan Thomas out loud; presents and more presents; he and his sister entertaining guests by acting out scenes from *Fawlty Towers*. And then at school: contraband cigarettes and *Viz* comics and house music, and poppers and beautiful boys in the showers. At school there was always something to take from someone who wouldn't miss it, someone who got what they deserved for being a fascist as well as a philistine.

These scenes of domestic life were all the more believable for being told in a sweltering room above the din of traffic by a drunken skeleton in a dingy, sweat-stained T-shirt.

It was Jasper he saw with his eyes closed. It was Bridey he saw everywhere else.

Walking through the East Village in the morning, early fall and the leaves turning gold, cutting through Tompkins Square and passing the queer cast-off kids sleeping out on the center lawn atop cardboard pallets beneath the trees, wearing everything they owned; or sitting groggy and pissed outside Ray's Candy Store with last night's bottle and a small hot coffee steaming into the cool air between their faces. It was impossible for Milo not to think of her.

When Jasper'd dragged her back from Larissis, she'd no money and looked rougher than they did: black hair, the kind of tan that comes from sleeping out. A feral thing with ice-blue eyes like an Eskimo dog's. She moved lightly, weighed nothing, had a delicate Celtic face, wide mouth, and pointed, slightly crooked eyeteeth. He'd many occasions to look at her.

Dressed always in Levi's and combat boots, her body was like a boy's: small breasts, might well have been pectoral muscles, her shoulders well-defined, veins visible in her strong arms. Bridey was an American survivor, the kind that made you think of the Donner Party. She had a rangy quick stride even when she was drunk; carried lighter fluid and matches and electrical tape in her bag. She smiled when she thought no one was looking and beneath her clothes the skin was soft and pale.

It had been twenty-five years since their last word, but when Milo moved to the United States he believed he would find her again. Stranger things had happened in the time they had known each other. Coincidences disguised as fate. She could be out on the street right now, could be sitting beneath the elms in Tompkins Square. The appointment at the New School had seemed like a sign. Another unlikely place she might know where to find him.

The job he'd had before this one was on a loading dock in Salford, not far from his mother's flat. Now he worked in a pretty building with wide corridors and tall windows. The hallway leading to his office was a gauntlet of closed wooden doors self-consciously decorated with worn, grubby *New Yorker* cartoons. He was obligated to be on campus every day to talk to students, to write his third collection, and to teach one class. The apartment he lived in was paid for by the school. It was, without doubt, the most luxurious situation he could tolerate.

Each day when Milo got to his office he made tea with an electric kettle, opened his laptop, and put on Joy Division or the Smiths. Read and deleted sentences he'd written the day before. Opened the window and let in the sounds of the street.

His students wore pajamas to class, emailed things he pretended not to receive. They were groomed and articulate and used to hearing themselves speak. All but four of them were white.

The shocking tranquillity of his life often left him dumb. And though it had yet to produce any results, he spent a good part of each day at his desk looking up Bridey's name and various guesses; sifting through the digital detritus, trying to piece together what had happened between then and now.

Bridey Sullivan

Bridey Sullivan fire

Bridey Sullivan hospital records, birth records, warrants

When he exhausted his search for her, he would occasionally look for himself, fascinated and disturbed by the violation of his private life and that, by virtue of writing and speaking and taking jobs, he'd lost the ability to be lost. The fact that his personal information was updated regularly enough to account for a position he'd accepted little more than a month ago shocked him. But the entries were not malign; instead, his life had been sanitized entirely, distilled into a product description. Wikipedia was the worst:

Milo Rollock

Milo Rollock (b. 1972) is an English writer and the author of two collections of poetry. He is currently Poet in Residence at the New School for Social Research in New York City.[1][3][6]

LIFE

Early years

Rollock grew up in Salford near the Irish Sea, the only child of Colleen Rollock, a garment worker.[3] His first collection, *In the Shadow of Machines*, is dedicated to his mother and contains several poems about working-class life. He has attributed his literary success to having "no television, no father, no money, nothing to do but read and fight."[1]

Education

Rollock dropped out of school at fourteen, began his training as a boxer at Longsight and Urmston and had a lackluster string of matches in Manchester and London in the mid-80s. Won 12 (KO 5) + lost 18 (KO 0) + draw 0 = 127 rounds boxed KO% 1.5.[5] In 1990, he received a full scholarship to University of Manchester on a special dispensation, where he studied metaphysical poetry, with a concentration in John Donne.

Career

In the Shadow of Machines won a Witter Bynner Poetry Prize in 1992 while Rollock was a sophomore in college.[12]

The *London Review of Books* called it "transcendent" and "lucidly brutal." The collection deals with themes of institutional violence, class, race, and gender. Despite these topics, it is apolitical in presentation.

The American publisher City Lights released his second volume, *Running*, the year of his graduation. It was translated into Portuguese, French, Turkish, and Greek.[7] After university, Rollock moved back to his hometown, worked in a shipyard, and returned to boxing, winning six matches over the course of a year. During this time he published only three poems, which ran in the *Paris Review*, the *Times Literary Supplement*, and the *London Review of Books*, respectively. Critics of Rollock's work have called him a token,[12,16] claiming his successes, particularly the Witter Bynner, were politically motivated and due to race.[11,12,16,43]

Running

Critically polarizing and more raw in form than *In the Shadow of Machines*, the long poem *Running* appears to be an account of Rollock's life on the street before he attended university. Told through the eyes of a teenage girl, clearly a stand-in for Rollock, the piece has been described as an ode and an indictment of the heroic tradition.[7]

Personal life

Rollock was the longtime partner of American painter Marc Lepson[23] and the subject of Lepson's well-known portrait series *Flight*.

If Milo was to believe the things he read, he'd had a full life. He'd written books and was once someone's "longtime partner." Was currently employed. The reality of his existence was footnoted, proven by articles in French and English and in newspapers of record. What he was afraid of, what compelled him to type his own name into the search engine, was finding details of the years between his lackluster career as teenage punching bag and the gracious dispensation that afforded him an education. The simple word Milo was afraid of reading was *Athens*.

The train jostled through the wasted landscape between cities. Scrub brush and spare rocky inclines visible in the distance, hills tufted with scorched grasses, and low mastic pines. I had stood in the aisle and held on to the seat Murat was facing, trying to get his attention.

I'd been running for Olympos for more than a month; had fallen into the routine of reading and riding trains and drinking, wandering the city with Jasper and Milo. I was already versed in the rivalries between hotels, in the bloody fights between taxi drivers and runners. Knew how to fold bills so it looked like I had more money in my hand, slip into the gates of the Parthenon unseen, to roam the ruins.

All along the train, people had pulled their windows down; trying to get some air, they were fanning themselves with leaflets other runners had given them. Murat, though, seemed unaware of the heat or the noise of conversations;

his feet were propped on a large duffel bag and he was read-ing a thin English translation of *The Clouds* by Aristophanes.

"Hi," I said for the second time.

He looked up and smiled, then his eyes went back to scan-ning the page, and soon he was lost again in reading. It made me want more than the book.

"Did you get to the part where they measure distances by how far a flea jumps?" I asked.

Murat was a shabbier version of the tourists who passed through every hour; had dark razor stubble, thick shiny hair flattened on one side from sleeping. He wore a short-sleeved button-down shirt with a frayed collar, looked like he'd been traveling a long way.

When he said nothing, I coughed. It was early, and I was drunk. I reached forward to touch the book, then put my hands in my pockets. I imagined he'd dozens more in his bag and felt capable of stealing all of them if he came back to the hotel with me.

"The part where they put Strepsiades under the blanket is good too," I tried.

This time he looked up and laughed. He had a contented, confident face; olive skin, long, thick eyelashes, darkest brown eyes.

"Are you studying classics?" he asked. The accent was jar-ring. Dutch, maybe German or Swedish; a mixed lilting sound, with round vowels and clipped consonants.

"No," I said, and handed him a leaflet. "Have you got somewhere to stay in Athens yet? Olympos is good, a few blocks from the station, and there's a view of the Acropolis."

"Oh, yeah?" he said.

"Essentially," I said. "More or less."

He looked at the leaflet. "Can you really stay here for two dollars?"

"That part's true," I said.

"I'll come, then."

For a moment I thought of sitting beside him for the rest of the trip, but I continued on into another car, crushed past people in the corridor, made my way to the bar and ordered an Amstel, which I drank in several long gulps, thinking about *The Clouds* and watching the countryside slip by. I thought about staying on the train when it reached Athens, so that I could keep going, so that I could see that new landscape that can only appear fully to you when you're alone. Stow on a boat, hitchhike a thousand miles, slide through customs and out the door into sunshine and some unintelligible culture. Not be able to ask for the time. Not know the word for water.

The door between cars jerked roughly, then slid open, and several more runners pressed into the space. Someone threw their leaflets into the air and they rained down upon us. Candy and Stephan, runners for a hotel called San Remo a few blocks from Olympos, looked around the car, leering in pleasure, all teeth, their pupils dilated nearly black. Candy was English, had short red hair, a gaunt acne-scarred face, and fat beautiful lips. Stephan might have been Dutch. He'd been traveling and sleeping out for years, had a flat tan face and bleached-blond hair, wore loose strands of beads around his neck, a Rod Stewart T-shirt, tight jeans and Greek sandals. They were ten years older than the rest of us, and vastly more accomplished at being gone.

"We killed the train!" Stephan yelled.

"Killed it," Candy said. "There's no one going home with you. There's no one ever going home with you again. This train goes directly to San Remo."

They stood kissing by the bar, holding cold bottles of Amstel against one another's necks.

Candy had told me once she had not killed her husband. That's not why she was in Athens, she said. Probably I'd heard different, but that's not what it was. She'd set his car on fire, she said. She'd cut his clothes to shreds, she'd given him a quarter of what he deserved. An eighth. But he was alive.

A tall German runner with moles on his face came to stand beside me, leaned against the wall. He wore a T-shirt that had a hole directly over his right nipple, tight black shorts, and ruined pointed shoes. He had knuckle tattoos, held a sweating bottle of beer.

"Where's the boys?" he asked.

I lit a cigarette, then shook my head, exhaling. "Sleeping."

"You're running this train all alone, then? How many you got?"

I didn't answer. "Who you running for now?"

"Argos," he said.

It was nicer than Olympos. The front was painted and it had a sign.

"You making money there?" I asked.

"A bit," he said. "This is my last run. I was hoping to see your boys before Friday."

"What's today?" I asked.

"Thursday."

It amazed me he knew something like that.

When I didn't ask him anything else, he said, "I'm going to Turkey."

"Oh, yeah?"

"Just going to check it out before I head to a kibbutz for work, then down to Africa; I have some friends in Nairobi."

"Doing what?"

"Living," he said.

We clinked bottles. Drank.

"If you're headed back through Europe," he said, "and want to stay in Berlin, there is a very good squat on Lychener Strasse. You can say I sent you."

"Okay," I said.

"Good shows in the neighborhood. No cops. I got a letter from a friend there—says it's like its own village now. There's under-the-table stuff in an antenna factory nearby. Maybe pub or kitchen work." He waded through the crowd to set his bottle on the bar instead of throwing it out the window, as was the custom, then returned with two more. When he passed me the Amstel I looked at his knuckle tattoos: an X, an eye, an infinity sign, a triangle inside a circle.

"To leaving," he said, raising the bottle.

"Always."

The train stopped in Athens, and he kept talking while he gathered a small crowd to take back to Argos. I paced along the tracks, looking for Murat, watching each little knot of tourists disembark, exhausted or excited. Bouzouki music played over the speakers mounted on the corners of the building. And people walked out into the heat, going separate places, headed on.

Candy and Stephan had amassed the largest crowd, college students on holiday: a group of drunken beefy teenagers, many of them Americans, wearing baseball hats.

Finally, Murat stepped down, adjusted his glasses, and scanned the crowd.

I walked over and held out my hand for his book bag.

"I'm Bridey," I told him. "Let me take your things."

N o one had come home to make dinner.

The rug was gritty, the electricity was on. I'd gotten through all the books in my room and started on theirs, took things home from the library. I lay on my back reading and eating crackers, distracted occasionally by the light of passing cars sliding across the ceiling and down the wall. They would be back later tonight, or in another couple of days. They would be back.

I should have been able to last longer, because there was enough food in the house; but I broke down after some weeks, panicked instead of taking care of it myself. I called him from the pay phone outside the library, and stared at a painted sign on the library window. It said AUGUST BOOKS and had a painting of a boat sailing over waves made of books. The phone rang and rang until the quarter dropped and I put it back in the slot and called again. All I said when he answered was "Hello." I couldn't say the rest.

When he got there I was sitting in the backyard, reading and watching my shadow stretch long on the grass. He would have come sooner, he said, but there was a fire burning and it couldn't be put out. They needed everyone, he told me, and even still it spread into the valley, down into the neighborhoods. Dare said I must have seen it on TV. I shook my head. The TV didn't work anymore.

I hadn't yet figured out we were leaving, so I went up to my room to read, but somehow he'd been up there before me. My things were put away in boxes and my dresser drawers were open.

"Ready?" He leaned his head through the doorway and smiled. "You got your stuff, Bone? Got all your books?" His voice sounded like he didn't use it much. "I'm sorry I left you waiting for so long," he said again.

I grabbed a carton of cigarettes off the empty bookcase. There was still a whole other carton in my parents' room but I didn't bother with it.

"How 'bout if you change out of your pajamas and put on some real shoes?" he asked.

"These are real shoes," I told him. They were the kind you used for walking in the water. My mother had bought them at the drugstore and they smelled bad if you took them off.

He picked me up and looked into my face. "Those are nice shoes, but how 'bout you put on some jeans and sneakers in case we want to stop and play somewhere."

"Where?"

"A park, maybe. Swings at the park or monkey bars."

He turned my dresser drawers upside down into the empty duffel he'd brought while I changed my clothes. We walked through the house together carrying my things. The screen door swung shut on its spring and we never went back there though my mother's dresses were still in the closet. And pictures of people we knew were stuck to the fridge with magnets shaped like letters, and a handful of change still sat on a table near their record player.

Dare had short hair and big arms, a scar on the bridge of his nose. His face looked pink in the light through the windshield.

"How old are you?" I asked him.

"Twenty-two," he said.

He said he'd already registered me for school. "We got a real nice place in Winthrop," he said. "We got the woods right close by; we got a pond. I'll be home when you get outta school, unless there's a jump I gotta do. It's a real good place, Bride, a real safe place. You're gonna like it there."

I wondered what had happened that made Dare so nice.

"Hell, you'll probably be the smartest kid in town, whatta you think? You're probably the smartest kid in whatever town this here one is we're driving through right now. You listening to me, Bridey?" He snapped his fingers in front of my face. "Bridey?"

In the car he talked about how fire breathes and eats, how he got caught in a tree and had to cut his chute away and beneath him he could see smoke rising from the forest bed like the fire had gotten inside the earth. He told me about looking down and seeing animals running fast through the trees, and fire spreading across the top branches like waves. He told me about finding an old cabin in a place that was burning; a man came out with a gun and said he would rather die in the blaze than leave the woods.

I couldn't envision the forest or the mountainside yet or the ocean. I'd lived in a town beside a highway with a shopping mall half an hour away and I'd never seen beautiful things. Dare asked if I remembered when he stayed with us to put plastic siding on the house. I didn't remember about the siding but remembered him coming for a visit and sitting in the yard with my mother; she was wearing a shirt the color of gray water with pictures of green apples on it, sitting in a folding chair. He told her jokes until she got a bellyache. I remember that he ordered Chinese food to be delivered and threw me up in the air and caught me, but apart from that I didn't remember anything at all and really I couldn't even remember what he looked like if I turned my head for a minute.

I smoked and tried to read.

Dare bummed a cigarette and clicked on the radio. The sun was shining. We turned off the highway and headed along a dirt road, and he said he was sorry again.

Then he hit the steering wheel with his fist, threw his cigarette out the window, grabbed mine and did the same.

"Jesus fucking Christ," he said. "What ten-year-old smokes?"

"I'm eleven."

"You do not smoke anymore, do you hear me? Bridey? How long you been in that house alone? Why didn't nobody come from school to check on you?"

"There's no school in summer," I told him.

"Why didn't you call nobody else? Why didn't you go to the neighbors or tell someone you needed help till I got there? Huh, Bridey? Answer me, Bridey."

"Because I didn't," I said.

Before she moved in, Declan stayed at Olympos often. Liked Jasper's wit, Milo's class. He would come by every week when he was in the city. Sometimes he'd disappear for months. Declan brought over packages of Papadopoulos cookies from the kiosk on Nissouru, and photos of places he'd visited: Nicaragua, Biafra, South Africa, Gaza.

Milo would look away, but Jasper would go through every one. Beautiful landscapes, coastal highways, smiling rugged people, tanks and jeeps and staging areas, guns, and bodies. Milo would hold a book in front of his face, busy himself washing their shirts in the sink.

"Oh, how lovely," Jasper would say. "Who's that, then, over there—one with the missing h—Oh, *these* chaps look friendly. What's that he's holding, dried fruit? Oh, an ear, is it? That's quite a big hole. Putting in a swimming pool? I see, and are there any *living* children in the area? Oh, here's one, I see. Not very lively, though, is he?

"All right, then, I think we'd like a fortnight package, something with a terrace overlooking the, ah . . . ditch full of limbs? Or maybe a private accommodation downwind from the mass grave. What do you think something like that would run?"

Declan had reached over and gently taken Jasper's wrist.

Even now, in the cloistered quiet of his office, Milo could feel the cold, sickening snap as if it were happening again.

Jasper gasped and shuddered, the photographs fell, and his arm flopped in the wrong direction, bone pressing against skin, his hand immobile.

Milo couldn't breathe.

"Now, that," Declan said, "is funny."

Olympos was unchanged; graying and sooty from proximity to the highway, paint peeling, the wrought-iron balconies crooked, threatening to fall. The front steps were cracked and the long glass doors opened into a cool cramped lobby at the bottom of a spiral staircase where Sterious sat stoop-shouldered and reading behind the front desk. He was wearing a polyester waffle-weave cardigan to fight the chill of the air-conditioning. I knocked on the glass and he hunched his shoulders, put his hand on top of his bald head, surprised but also miming surprise—then motioned for me to come in.

Sterious loved company. He worked reception in the mornings and afternoon, sipping Greek coffee made in a narrow gold pot he kept on a hot plate behind the desk. Every afternoon two men who wore rings and a tall woman with blond hair who worked in the neighborhood would visit him to play dominoes and drink ouzo. The woman wore sunglasses, sweatpants, and terry-cloth slippers. I wouldn't have recognized her at night beneath the red bulb a few doors down except for her laugh.

Jasper and Milo and I would often sit with Sterious in the lobby, especially if we'd run out of money for drinks.

"Bridey!" he shouted, getting out two demitasse glasses from behind the desk. "Where you went all this time?"

In the cool of the lobby my head felt clearer, but I could smell my own sweat, the days of sleeping out on the boat and before that a few nights in a park. I leaned against his desk while he poured us some shots.

"Seeing the sights," I said.

"What sights?"

"Oh, I don't know; the Eiffel tower, Disneyland, the Pyramids, the Great Wall of China. That kind of thing."

"No Stonehenge?"

"*And* Stonehenge."

"No Berlin Wall?" He poured himself more ouzo.

"*And* the Berlin Wall. I wrote your name on it. I wrote 'Sterious Hatzipanagis was here.' But I think it's not long for this world."

"And you got married?"

"I *did* get married. I married a race car driver, but it didn't work out."

"No, no, no—a race car driver? Too selfish."

He poured me another shot. There was an ashtray on the desk that had been in our room; in the bottom of it a picture of Pan teaching Daphnis to play the flute. I looked up to meet his eyes.

"I remember you was skinnier before," Sterious said, reaching into his sweater pocket and pulling out a fistful of pistachios, pressing them into my hands. "Maybe shorter too."

"Anything happen while I was gone?" I asked.

He leaned in to confide. "Yes. I decided Milo is not so much like a man. You first think what a big, strong man. But he is like a girl. You know how a girl is—she think about things, think for a long time about things and maybe cry sometimes? And he's pretty like a girl, no? Even with that punched ear."

"Milo's here?" I asked.

"I don't mean you're not a girl for you don't cry," he said. "Or for your clothes," he added.

"Thanks. Is Milo here?"

He shook his head. "I don't know where he is." He waved his hand, dismissing it all. "Nothing happened while you were gone." He opened the desk drawer and took out the key to room thirty-one and a couple drachma notes, set them before me. "Catch the 309," he said. "It's a big train, and to-night, many, many beds empty. You come back just in time!"

"Were you here when Jasper left?"

He didn't answer. Handed me a pile of leaflets; pictures of a hotel I'd never seen before, with the words *Get Ready to Be Amazed!* printed across the top and room rates listed on the bottom. The most expensive room was seven dollars. You could sleep on the roof for fifty cents. The only people who ever stayed at Olympos were poor, hiding, prone to risk. Or

else they were easy marks: travelers unaware of how danger-
ous the neighborhood was.

"Sterious," I said, "did Jasper leave anything here for me?"

He shook his head, said nothing.

"When did Milo leave?" I asked. "Did he give you anything
to give me?"

"No."

"You remember Murat?" I asked. "I was wondering——"

"No," he said.

"Murat Christensen. You remember him."

"No," he said.

"C'mon, man," I said. "He stayed here. He lived here."

"I'm happy you're back," Sterious said.

The spiral stairs ended at the abandoned top floor. The
claustrophobic heat in our old room was overwhelming. I
opened the balcony door to get a cross breeze and let in the
air and noise from the street. The ceiling was high, molded
tin, painted blue. The walls were yellow and peeling, the
floor tiles patterned in a blue and white meander, a wrought
iron balcony was full of dirt and crushed glass and overlooked
the highway.

Our bed was pushed up against the wall, and there was a
smaller cot in the opposite corner where Declan had sometimes slept, a small white sink with a mirror above it too high
for me to see myself in, and a flimsy chest of drawers. I
looked beneath the beds for any artifact Jasper might have
left: books, a T-shirt, maybe money, a letter. I tore the sheets
from the bed and pushed the flimsy wooden dresser aside,

took out the drawers, and turned them over. We'd had dozens of books; Milo always had a blue spiral-bound notebook to write in. When I'd left, the place had been packed with things Jasper bought or lifted or insisted we get from the flea market. But now there was nothing.

I turned my face to the pillow and breathed deeply, hoping for that medicinal mix of licorice and mud and bitter flowers: their smell, distinct and intoxicating.

This was the room where we'd slept together. The room that had spun beneath us while we played gin and hearts. Where we'd sit at night in our underwear getting up to drink from the short tap in the cracked sink. The hush of traffic going by sounded like an ocean. We read aloud to each other and ate bread we'd stolen from the bakery on Nissouru Street. We washed our clothes in the sink with bar soap and hung them on the balcony to dry, and at night we walked across the city and up into the hillside paths where the trunks of the trees were painted white, to sit by the base of the Acropolis and see the sprawl of lights stretch back until they reached the empty dark where hills rose. We wandered until there was no one out beneath the haunted glow of distant morning but people to fear.

And this was the room to which we returned, where everything looked silver, pale gray sky shining in, spilling through the balcony doors and washing over us. That light laid itself down upon our skin and in the wetness of our eyes; illuminated sweat-darkened hair, faces, mouths, collarbones, a lip tucked beneath a lip; revealed the limbs and lines of a body traced back to the shadowed places of another: the back of a knee, the curve of a hand, a fist closed around a wrist or an ankle, closed around flesh that fit perfectly in the cradle between fingers and palm.

I remembered how fine their hands looked clasped in the silver light while they slept. Their cheeks upon the pillow when it was over and morning came at last, turning the sky the color of an old bruise.

M ilo had been staring at the doorway from his desk for a good thirty seconds before he noticed Paul, in his tweeds, standing in the hallway speaking.

"Sorry?" he asked. "Haven't had me cuppa."

"I said, 'How are you settling in?'" Paul smiled, he had pale, deep-set eyes and the kind of eyelashes that made Milo think he must have once been ginger-haired. His skin was elastic and well-hydrated, wavy white hair touching his shoulders.

Milo made himself say "Wonderful" twice. Paul was firmly solicitous in the way of people who've paid you to do things.

"Looking forward to hearing your students' work at the party tonight," he said heartily.

"Should be quite something," Milo said, as though this weren't the first he'd heard of it. He could smell the crisp odor of laundry and cologne and toothpaste that radiated from Paul, and tried not to watch the man take in his office.

The desk was covered with his own work; there were open books on the floor beside his chair, an empty bookcase, a plate on the windowsill containing cigarette butts, and a dry crusty pile of used Barry's tea bags. He'd found a reliable supply of Barry's gold blend, in McNulty's on Christopher Street, the only decent shop in a neighborhood which should be consumed in a fatal fire. In any case, the used tea bags had nowhere to go, because the trash bin was filled with crushed tallboys of Four Loko supplied to him by his very best student, Tiffany Navas. They were in there because the recycling container was overflowing with student work. Paul raised his eyes to Milo's and smiled without much feeling.

"Well, fantastic," Paul said. "I'm bringing my *wife* tonight; she's a fan. You know, when we *met* . . ." He looked off in the distance with a studied, wistful smile. "You'll love this, actually . . . She was *living* in this little postage stamp–sized *apartment* down on Orchard Street, I remember the first time I went over there, she showed me this copy of *In the Shadow of Machines.* Honest to God. And it was *so* dog-eared and *so* annotated, it was practically falling apart. I told her to bring it tonight, thought you might get a kick out of seeing it. Plus she's dying for you to sign it."

"Oh, how lovely," Milo said. "Of course."

"Oh, hey, just a minor thing." Paul touched his hand lightly to his beard. "Don't know if you *knew*. If you're not checking your *email*—you know, don't feel like checking whatever; I totally get what a pain that stuff can be—but just FYI, there's a *mailbox* in the department office with your name on it and there's hard copies there of things you might need. And you know Deb or myself would be happy to help you set up your, ah . . . faculty email account if you need help with that, too, just to help you catch up, maybe, on some of the bureaucracy. So just let us know."

"Of course," Milo said. "Yes. Thank you. I shall be sure to stop in later today and see her."

"Great. Again, no big deal, just, uh, some attendance things to sign off on and, ah, a couple other questions Deb had, forms for direct deposit . . . that, uh . . . not quite sure. But whatever, whenever you get to it. Okay. We'll catch you tonight." He gave a wry well-practiced smile and tapped the doorframe twice before heading down the hall.

Milo got up to shut the door, then put his headphones on and turned out the light.

When next he looked up, the shadowy vision of Navas was standing in his office, her arms folded. She snapped on the light, pulled his headphones down around his neck, stacked the papers that were covering his desk, and dropped them heavily to the floor.

"Why didn't you tell me there was some special thing tonight?" he asked her.

"What thing?" She sat where the papers had been, lit her cigarette with his lighter, then put it in her pocket. "Oh, the *reading*? *You're* the one wrote it on the fucking blackboard

Monday. You can't remember? No more Four Loko for you, Professor."

"I'm afraid, Ms. Navas, there will indeed be more Four Loko for me, especially if we are to attend this mystery event."

Milo tried not to favor Tiffany Navas when the semester began, but had given up about three weeks in. Her work was simply better than her peers', her skin darker, her accent richer. And she was more intelligent; could look around the room and size up the people in it fast as any runner. No one was taking care of Navas; she was taking care of herself. She didn't show up to class wearing pajama pants and flip-flops, or a lanyard of keys around her neck like a giant baby in danger of getting lost. Did not talk about her parents or pets or family vacations, did not have conversations about television. Never wore a baseball cap. And, best of all, when they announced they were taking Four Loko off the market, she and her friends bought several dozen cases. Four Loko was a malt liquor made with caffeine, alcohol, and wormwood. It was poorman's freebase, white-trash absinthe. Because of her foresight, Navas was able to supply the beverage on very little notice, with a great profit to herself. She also did not care about the no-smoking policy. Navas was tall and fleshy and wore shiny deep-red lipstick.

"I don't got that much left, anyway," she said, her long black hair falling forward, disturbing the room with the faint smell of vanilla musk. "You're gonna hafta start drinking Red Bull and schnapps like every other loser. Listen, we'll go to this thing and then you come up t'the Bronx an see my brother fight this guy, okay?"

"What did the guy do?"

"Nothing."

"Maybe," Milo said.

"That's where the Four Loko is," she said.

"Then yes," he said. "I shall be delighted."

I woke up alone in the dark, tangled in sheets, sweat soaked, nauseated, my face in Jasper's pillow, memories of him thick and suffocating in the little room.

Shadows played across the ceiling, and for a moment I thought it might be morning already and that I missed the train I was supposed to run.

I walked unsteadily to the sink and threw up, splashed cold water on my face, rinsed out the basin, then wet my head and neck, brushed my teeth out on the balcony, and watched the sun get lower in the sky, filling me with the hollow dread that comes from waking up sober at dusk. I'd made a mistake coming back.

The Athens I'd left was crawling with police. The Athens I'd returned to was eerily calm. I didn't want to go out— didn't want to ride the train and see other runners—but there was little choice if I was to keep sleeping indoors. I grabbed my lighter and pile of leaflets, ran down the spiral staircase through the lobby and out onto the street.

Down on the pavement the air was finally beginning to cool, streetlamps and headlights were turning on, the sky was a rich haunting gaslight blue. The air and the night were working upon me, and with every step I took toward the station I felt more hopeful and alive. I crossed the highway, cut across the scrub-grass park and then through the back gate to the platform of Larissis Station, where bouzouki music played over the loudspeakers, and I stood waiting to board a train headed west.

Runners were sitting facing the tracks, their backs against the smooth brick wall. Bigger hotels, like Athens Connection and Luzani, sent out better-dressed, more serious runners than the rest of us; they sat apart like commuters or tourists, carried binders with actual photographs of rooms, bars, dining areas. Unlike our photos, these were not stock images. These runners didn't smile at anyone who didn't mean commission, didn't raise their voices, didn't share the drunken bond between transients who'd made their way to the city and were happy to find work. They were there to fill their hotels and get paid. *Professional runner* was the epithet. They walked onto the train and walked off with every rich person on it, taking a shuttle straight to their hotels.

For the rest of us, running was about waiting. Waiting for the train, then waiting for it to get you there, waiting for the drink to be served, waiting for the alcohol to take effect. Idling, not running. When Jasper was there, the waiting was better. Boxes came from London addressed to him, full of books by Pushkin, Turgenev, and Nabokov, blank notebooks and pens and *Viz* comics. A semiregular care package with no note, no money—or none that we knew about. When we asked who sent these things, he'd say "A friend" or "A teacher" or simply "A man I know." Sometimes we sat on the train and read, there and back, didn't talk to anyone at all—just took the hotel's money, watched the countryside drift past from the window. Got off the train long enough to eat a souvlaki at Elefsina and came home to read and drink and wander some more.

A group of taxi drivers walked on to the platform from the back gate and it grew quiet. I thought about stepping into the station to stay away from them or going back to the hotel, but my need for money won out.

I dropped my cigarette and stepped on it, watched Takis, a tall, beefy man with hairy arms wearing a black sailor's cap, walk down the center of the platform pushing and shoving some skinny kid in sneakers and shorts who was keeping his head down and trying to get out of his way.

The other drivers stood in a group by the back gate, smoking.

Sick of the shoving, the kid eventually turned around and put his back to the wall. It was Tom, a South African boy who ran for San Remo, and was usually high on hash. Takis stood in front of him, rested one hand on the wall, and leaned in close. Tom gave him a coy smile, leaned forward with his lips parted, and closed his eyes as if he were lifting his face for a kiss.

The laughter was immediately broken by the popping sound his head made when it hit the wall. Tom's hands flew out, instinctively trying to break whatever fall might be coming, but he lost consciousness first; buckled, crumpled to the platform, his mouth bleeding. A cry went up from the runners, and someone began screaming for the station cop who would never show up.

Then a whole crowd—maybe fifteen other drivers—came from the back gate, moved in on us, laughing, shoving, and grabbing runners who were trying to stay away from the edge of the tracks. Bouzouki music played over the loudspeaker.

I couldn't see far down the platform and couldn't hear well over the music and shouting. I crouched lower behind a bench, pulled out a cigarette, and smoked it lying low, staring into the tangle of rushing legs and fists. I knew there was no crawling around the corner into the station without getting stomped.

Directly in front of me, a driver grabbed a kid I didn't know by the hair and was pulling his head back. The kid was screaming in a way I hated, his eyes strained, like a frightened deer, bulging, whites showing, searching for any way out. Another runner tried to pull the driver away from behind, but he turned and punched that boy hard in the nose. I was surprised it made such a loud noise, and that the driver'd managed to keep hold of the other kid's hair while doing it. The boy with the broken nose was trying to push his way through the crowd. But I knew he would end up falling before he reached the gate.

Bottles were smashed on the ground. To my left a puddle of blood was forming, streaming darkly across the platform toward the tracks. Everywhere there was cursing and angry panicked yells for the station cop who would never come. I watched Stephan getting trampled by sandaled and booted feet on the cement. He rolled over and covered his head with his arms, raised his knees to protect his stomach. I watched while two men kicked him in the back and stomped his legs. Candy was nowhere to be seen.

Declan came in at the northern edge of the platform, took in the scene, then pushed quickly through the crowd, weaving easily around bodies.

A brief hush fell as he walked up behind Takis and punched him square in the back of the head, knocking him off balance and sending him to the concrete with a flat smack. No one moved.

The train rolled in with a wrenching squeal of brakes, bringing tourists and commuters. A conductor leaned out one of the doors, blowing his whistle and calling for the station cops. Several people ventured off the train, running clumsily for the shelter of the station. A tall, gangly kid got elbowed in the neck and fell to the ground beneath the weight of his heavy pack. A few runners tripped over him and scrambled to get up. The conductor continued to blow his whistle from the door of the train. A few yards away from me, another runner got knocked into the bricks, leaving the wall wet with his blood.

Declan had Takis on the ground.

He stepped back quickly and kicked him several times in the gut and ribs, pausing slightly each time as if he were thinking about stopping but couldn't. Finally he walked away, sat back down and sighed, looked at his watch. His face settled into a patient disappointed scowl.

Takis didn't move. Drivers came over to see if they could pull him up, got him to a kneeling position. His face was red and puffy and streaked with sweat and blood; the other drivers waited for him to stand before strutting awkwardly to the gate, hurt but with shoulders thrown back, bearing the weight of Takis. One of them was cut badly, a dark stain blooming on the front of his shirt.

Greek music still playing inside the station and out on the platform, which was covered with glass and bloody footprints and leaflets, runners sitting on the ground or standing exhilarated and bewildered.

"You're cut," Declan said.

I shook my head.

"Here," Declan said. "Let me look at that."

"I'm fine."

"Don't be a fucking muppet. There's blood all over your arm. Let me *look* at it."

I checked to see if I might have a nosebleed, then saw it covering my T-shirt and shoulder, dripping down my arm into my hand. "It's not mine," I said.

He grabbed me by the wrist and pulled me along the platform into the men's room, ran water over my arm. It felt good and exposed no cut. The shirt was soaked and spattered red and I took it off and threw it in the wire garbage can near the sink.

He said, "God, you're skinny, lass. You're a little bone." The words echoed off the tile, reverberated farther than the confines of the room.

"Sterious said I gained weight."

"Man's a gobshite, isn't he?"

I glanced at my reflection in the warped steel plate bolted to the bricks, then looked away. Declan squinted, leaned forward, his face close to my body.

"What's that?" he asked.

I folded my arms over my chest. "My tits."

I watched his eyes follow the line of my body, watched him find the outline of the lighter fluid canister tucked into the front pocket of my shorts. Then he looked into my eyes for a gleaming frozen second. There's a way you're supposed to act around certain animals, making sure they know you're not afraid, holding your hand out for them to smell. I dropped my arms, relaxed my shoulders, stood before him in the dank stench of the tiled room, until he tossed me his jean jacket to wear.

"Thanks," I said, rolling up the sleeves.

He nodded. "It'll save you the embarrassment of your mates finding out you're really a fourteen-year-old boy."

Runners were getting on the train to Elefsina. I could see them through the windows, crowding the aisles. I ran along the platform as the train lurched into motion, caught the bar, and jumped onto the step as it gained speed. Declan hopped up after me with ease.

"Watch your step, Bridey," he said.

My uncle's voice said: "Bone."

It said: "Hey, Bone. Wake up. Wake up, Bone, let's get going."

His hands lifted my foot into the air, straightened the toe of my sock, then jammed my sneaker on. A stab of pain at my Achilles tendon where the blisters were said it was really morning.

"C'mon, Little Sullivan. Wake the fuck up." He snapped on a light.

"I'm awake," I said.

"Open your eyes, then."

He pulled me into a sitting position, shook me. Dare was wearing sweats and a tight gray T-shirt. And so was I, dressed that way for bed so I wouldn't have to get up ten minutes earlier. He knelt before me, brusquely tying my sneakers, then stood and stretched. It was still dark outside, silent, shadows of tall trees against the window. My glow-in-the-dark monster models gave off a fading green light from on top of the bookcase.

In the bathroom I hunched and drank water and tried to rest my feet by leaning against the sink. I opened the medicine cabinet, got out rubber bands for my hair and white tape for my blisters. My ankles hurt when I touched them.

The lights were bright in the living room and his helmet and gear were in a pile by the door next to his go bag.

"Is there a fire?" I asked.

Dare didn't answer. He said, "Get it together," clapped his hands sharply. "Let's go. Move on out."

We stepped off the sloping wooden porch and ran along the narrow path beside the house, past the pond and out on to the hard dirt road. The forest loomed, crested blue and deep in the distance, a fading moon was still in the sky and the pale light of morning rose silvery pink against the trees. The birds were beginning to wake and sing. The air was sweet and clear with the smell of pine and grass from our meadow.

Our sneakers crunched along toward the turnoff that would lead to the track behind school. It didn't matter if I kept up with him or not, but I still had to finish five miles. The temperature was cool and perfect and the sky brighter every minute, and I ran fast because when you got going there was no more pain, even when your feet were bleeding.

"Is there a fire?" I asked again, my heart pounding, beginning to sweat in the cool air, my body feeling fine and strong like I could lift off the ground, like I could fly. Dare ran with an easy cadence like he weighed nothing, and I tried to catch up to him, to beat him.

When I got close he grabbed me up, spun me around, ran backwards holding me like a training weight, then dropped me down to run beside him, holding my hand for a moment so I had to sprint to keep up.

"There is always a fire, little Bone," he called to me over his shoulder. "Nothing in this world is put here to stay."

Summer months and fall he was away all the time. In winter we would hole up and light the woodstove. He went to the jump base nearly every day while I was at school. In the early days when I was living there he'd be waiting when I got home, or sometimes down in the basement making sure things were in order.

There were kids at school I talked with but most of them didn't live nearby. I did homework out of boredom. Practiced throwing darts, built card houses, read. When I was younger I hunkered down on the rug and drove Matchbox cars through the yellowed landscape of nuclear holocaust and crumbs beneath the couch. Imagined being the only person left alive, wandering through an empty city. You have to be strong to be one of the last people on earth. Strong enough to see if there are other survivors. Strong enough to live alone for years, looking.

Dare and I went snowshoeing and skiing in the Methow Valley, skated on the frozen pond. Ate deer and rabbit and salmon that he cooked on the narrow gas stove in the low-ceilinged kitchen. When I was older we went hunting. And in the evenings he talked about the government. What they're going to do. And about the forest, the mountainside, about defending the life of trees and earth and ocean from the stupid things people did. But I knew it wasn't really about the earth. The earth was fine no matter what, would be even better when we were gone—that was obvious. The things he talked about were only considered wrong because they made it bad for people, made the world uglier or poisoned the water and made them sick. Or made them feel bad about the dead animals that they had loved killing in the first place. The people who cared were just like the people who didn't. Afraid to die, and pretending they never would. Whether you fought that fear by destroying a forest or preserving it didn't really matter. Once we were gone, all the pretty views would be restored.

Some of Dare's stories I knew by heart: the campers they hoisted from a blaze with a helicopter, their son already unconscious from smoke; the way the fire looks at night, and the way the forest looks after—like a haunted world, a painting of hell—trees transformed to black, gnarled stones.

By the time I began high school—or attended the minimum days required to be considered a student—I was a different girl. Strong and strange from living in the country; raised on tales of survival, running, and hunting. Watching Dare turn the basement into a second home where we'd live after the missiles rained down.

Running

The kids at school feathered their hair back and wore turtlenecks with little pictures of spouting whales on them; bought different-colored rubber bands for their braces. They played on teams. Ordered things from the L.L.Bean catalog. Talked about their family lineages like being dead was some big honor. Other kids lived in trailers or new one-story HUD houses. Some of those boys ran and hunted like I did. But nobody had a bunker under their house. Nobody liked being alone as much as I did. Nobody was as interested in fire.

One did not observe Bridey, Milo thought. She observed you. Something inside her did, a regal solitary thing that compelled you to act on its behalf. She'd an air of resignation about her, like she was abiding the real world and might decide to get rid of it altogether.

At night or early in the morning when Jasper'd fallen asleep, Bridey and Milo would stay up and talk; the balcony door open and the sound of the street echoing in the high-ceilinged room, Jasper's pale body lying sated between them.

Shouts echoed up from the street, then a woman's angry voice. Far away the minor notes of an ambulance siren stretched past like the bridge of "Somewhere over the Rainbow," then faded into the distance. Bridey laid her head on Jasper's chest while he slept.

"That's the sound of them taking Jasper away," she said, smiling faintly, hair matted from being ground into the mattress.

"To where?" Milo asked.

"Anywhere," she said, her eyes closed. "Where is good?"

Milo slid his thigh over Jasper's and propped himself up on an elbow to look at her. It was getting cooler. The shape of her collarbone was set shining against the hollow shadows.

"The sea."

"Where he can live with the other mermen." She ran her short, dirty nails over Jasper's skin and he stirred, breathed heavily in his sleep. Then she reached across and found Milo's hand, wove her fingers between his.

"Why are you here?" she asked.

The question startled him. There were many reasons and he was sure she knew them all. Jasper's voice, her strange face. The heat of day. The warm sustained painlessness of drink. The music on the platform. The feeling that everything had already ended and this was the place you go after it's over. He was there for the sound of Jasper's breathing, his mouth, his cock. Her eyes upon them. Everything a symbol, a shape replacing the thought that created it. All the words they'd swallowed, the words they couldn't say. He knew it was the drug of their bodies had him thinking like that night after night. The nearly invisible down on the back of Jasper's neck had poisoned him. Why was he here? Who would look after Jasper, he thought, if he wasn't?

The crowd on the train was louder than usual. People were excited, recounting the fight. I walked down the aisle with Declan and continued on through the connecting cars to the bar, ordered a pint, drank it in a few long gulps, and gave the bottle back to the bartender, asking for another, then pulled a pack of crushed cigarettes from my back pocket, tried to straighten them for a few seconds before tearing the filters off and throwing them to the sticky floor. I smoked with loose tobacco on my tongue while the countryside flew by. On the outskirts of Athens a golden-white light emanated from a foundry, briefly illuminating the industrial landscape and the twisted silhouettes of olive trees in the distance, then there was nothing but darkness. Behind me a crush of runners, some with blood-streaked faces, were singing a footballers' song. I looked over and saw that one of them was wearing a pair of Jasper's shorts.

No one was sober by the time we reached Elefsina. Close

to twenty runners were already waiting for the 309 outside a little shack that served as the station house, passing around bottles of retsina and Metaxa and talking. I sat down next to some British kids who said the train would be half an hour late.

One of the drunk boys I'd talked to in Drinks Time just that morning asked when I'd gotten back to town, then handed me a bottle and rolled the screw cap back and forth in his hands nervously.

"Today," I told the blond-haired oaf, drinking from his Metaxa.

"You hear about Jasper and that black kid?"

"No," I said, to see if his story had changed. "What happened?"

"They were your mates, weren't they?"

"No."

"They were poofs, you know?" he laughed.

I looked at him, took another drink.

"Jasper y'could see, but that other kid a bender? Jesus fuck, nah. Th'man's huge."

"So what happened?"

"They were queers."

"Did something happen to them?"

"I told you," he said. "They were fucking each other in the arse."

I rested the back of my head on the bench.

I could hear Declan's voice saying, "We had to mutilate them. After we saw what they did to those nuns, we couldn't let . . ." Could be the punch line to a joke, could be something he did last week.

"When are you going back to London?" the kid beside me asked.

"I'm not," I said. "I'm not from London. Why can't people hear my accent?"

"Maybe you haven't got one," he said.

I squinted down the tracks.

"He starved to death," the boy said suddenly. "That's right, that was it, I remember that. But it was probably AIDS, right? Died after they found that Muslim piker hiding in one of the hotels. Or just before, maybe. Someone called his parents and they came and got him."

I felt I might gag. Stood up quickly. The liquor was blazing through me, making me numb, and I stumbled closer to the station house and leaned against it.

In the dim light, the little platform and shack and the gawky blond vagrants passing bottles looked like a painting from a century ago, or documentary footage of migrant workers: ragged people sitting together, thin, drunk, and fed on crumbs, smiling in the lamplight.

The strong smell of Turkish coffee drifted out from the station house. Someone passed me a fifth of Mastika, and I had no intention of sharing it. Then Declan came out of nowhere to block my view of the pretty scene.

"A bunch of fucking clowns here tonight," he said. "We'll kill this train ourselves."

"To killing"—I raised the bottle—"and to Elefsina," I said.

"Home of the lesser mysteries." I took a long drink, then poured some drops on the ground in case everyone I loved was dead and couldn't get their hands on ethanol in the afterlife. I was in the middle of my second toast when Declan grabbed the bottle from me and threw it onto the tracks.

"Keep it together," he said.

A German kid from Hotel Larissia started the third verse of "Deutschland, Deutschland über alles" but was dropped by a hard punch to the gut, then kneed in the face when he hunched over. More blood, more laughter.

A Scottish boy named Mike jumped onto a bench and sang in a fussy staccato: "My. Name. Is Joseph. Gunnar. And. I work. For. Connection. I won't. Drink. Your. Metaxa. For I'm. A pro-fes-sional. Run-ner."

He rolled the R's dramatically, making the words sound especially silly. I remembered liking Mike. He and Jasper had tried to start a currency exchange scam, which lasted a day. Mike looked robust, one of the few runners who filled out his clothes. He had bad teeth, dark eyes, and wavy dirty-blond hair; he was cleanly shaved. Mike had spent one month in Athens and one month on the islands for the past five summers, came with money, ran to pay for his drinks, then went home. A poor man's holiday.

"My name is Bridey Sullivan," he sang in a puzzling approximation of a Danish accent I didn't have. "I come for a drunken dead man."

Funny enough. A few people looked at me out of the corners of their eyes.

Mike's eyes were shiny and sentimental from drink as he stepped off the bench, walking toward me, trying to bring an image of Jasper up between us.

"Just taking the piss," he said. "You know he'd be laughing." He offered me a cigarette, took one for himself.

"It's okay," I said. I stepped back to look at his face, then kicked him hard in the balls with the heel of my boot.

Mike gave a little shriek, sucked in a mouthful of air, crouching, one hand reaching toward the ground. More laughter, clapping, someone yelled, "Atta girl."

I hadn't considered kicking him until it was already happening, until I'd raised my knee and felt my throat constrict and a chill on my back. I looked down at him, searching for the remains of any emotion. His shoulders and back were nicely defined beneath his thin T-shirt. Everything about the way he crouched there was lovely. His hair was darker at the roots and I could see the paleness of his scalp and the back of his neck, his freckled skin. His sneakers were coming apart. I admired him as he knelt where he belonged, then wandered back along the gravel path to wait for the train.

Dare kept large metal canisters of gasoline in the basement. You pumped the top to pour fuel into smaller containers. I got a metal canteen from the kitchen and filled it with gasoline and then went hiking. I'd walked these trails with Dare for a whole year. When I was younger I'd pretend I was scoping out a place to build my own house. But that's not what I wanted anymore.

The hillside was steep, and I turned to look down on our low ranch house and the rich algae green of the pond. I'd been paying attention to Dare, been reading about wind shifts. Just in the time we lived there, fires had swallowed houses and hillsides. It was mostly men who made the fires and the conditions for the fires and then men put them out. It wasn't a way to live.

I chose a place where the forest met the green of the hillside, a little shadowed valley before a dark curtain of trees, a calm cover for animals and birds. I sloshed the gasoline from the canteen all over the base of an old tree maybe hundreds of years old, rooted to and rising from an earth that was older still. I'd been alive for just thirteen years and I could wreck it. Send it back to wherever I'd come from, to wherever my parents had gone. It was exciting, like standing at the ocean and looking out at nothing, the invisible force of wind in your face, pushing salt air into your lungs.

I got out the box of strike anywhere matches, lit one and watched the yellow flame gutter in the wind, then dropped it on the tree. The flame undulated like liquid, shot, wriggling up the trunk like blood traveling in a vein, blue and electric, the tips yellow and pouring black smoke. It made me jump on to my toes. I could feel it through the core of my body.

The bark popped and crackled with little sparks. And I held my hands in tight fists. Unless the branches caught and the leaves burned it would soon go out. But it was fall and there were plenty of dry leaves; the trunk was already turning black. I waited, breathing in the smell of the tree's life as it was extinguished by the fire, feeling the rush of heat and a tremendous ecstatic shudder. I had not felt so good and so sad in a very long time. It was like my mother singing to me at night. I put my arms out in an empty embrace. Then ran, tumbling down the hillside, the fire at my back, blackening the tall grass, sending up ash and sparks that hovered and scattered around me like a luminous swarm.

* * *

I expected Dare to be gone when I got home later that day, or to be there talking about the fire. I expected him to say something. But he was watching television. The fire was too small. No one had to come from the sky to put it out. The Volunteer Fire Department sent one guy in a pickup truck. And I had to stay where I was.

The evening was murder. Ten students relentlessly read their poetry, eight and a half of them completely without talent. Milo was dying for a cigarette the entire time, ready to weep by the end of the hour. One student's work comprised texts sent back and forth between him and a girl, which he read off his mobile in a deliberately bored monotone, to the great amusement of his peers.

How, he thought, for fuck's sake, could anyone possibly have the arrogance to believe their lives as the disgruntled chattel of "good families" and "fine institutions" would make for interesting literature? Instead of producing an endlessly trite chronicle of suburban privileges and petty privations, or fantasies drawn from the shallowest well. Fucking skimming bastards every one.

That night was not the first he had seen Navas as his Beatrice: angelic, holding a luminous can of Four Loko in her hand.

She elbowed him sharply after the last poem was read and they applauded, said hasty good-byes. Skipped down the steps and up Third Avenue, making their way to Union Square, ran down into the close hollow of the station. A marvel of steel and tile and tracks and grime and noise; the screech of breaks and dozens of automatic doors shutting at once; the recording of a hyperarticulated white man's voice ringing out in perfect American: *"Ladies and gentleman if you see a suspicious object on the subway or platform alert a police officer or an MTA employee. If you see something say something"*; bodies pushing past, paths crossing.

A shirtless man covered in glitter with a towel on his head draped behind him like long tresses danced and whirled along the platform, wearing a cardboard crown. A boy, maybe fifteen years old, with stumps for arms, drumsticks duct-taped where his hands would be, played a tight ska beat on a plastic ten-gallon drum.

They crammed into the car, pressed flat against strangers smelling of sweat and cologne and hand sanitizer.

"You should have read," Milo said.

"You got my work; I don't need to stand up there for them."

"You do need to," he said. "Did I seem bollixed? Paul already thinks I'm a waster."

"I don't know what the fuck 'bollixed' is but you were really good to those poet-dude bros. Got that Professor Rollock *look* you give them so they think they did something all meaningful and shit."

He loved her laugh, a sharp "*Ha*," and then she would throw her head back and inhale and laugh harder. "Oh, Christ," she said. "What the fuck was that poem Seth did about walking through the 'grit-ty ci-ty st-reets.' *Every* fucking stanza starts with 'I wanna tell her.' I'm, like, 'Dude, *seriously?*' 'I wanna tell her about the stars, about the red leaves.' *Stupid*est bullshit ever . . . He *actually* said 'I wanna tell her about the *stars*' . . . That's '*wanna*,' not 'want to.' Please. The affectation."

"It wasn't bad because it was 'bout looking at stars, like," Milo told her, "or because he used a repetitive device, or the argot of our time. Those things can be done well."

"Just not by that guy," she said. "And motherfucker's got soooo much to tell her. Girlfriend had a lobotomy, I guess. She doesn't know what the fuck she's even looking at."

"There's got to be a way you can teach that class instead of me," Milo said.

"When have I got time to be a teacher? I'm taking eighteen credits and working at Macy's. Plus fuck that. Look what it's done to you in just a month."

Most of the white people had cleared out of the car around Eighty-Sixth Street with their handbags and close shaves and nice suits. Milo and Navas rode for half a dozen more stops, sitting side by side on the light-blue seats, looking at the advertisements for plastic surgery and community colleges. The cheerful voice of authority reminded them that a crowded subway car is no excuse for sexual misconduct, and to remain alert and have a safe day.

Streetlamps were just turning on when the train emerged from belowground into the dusky flame-blue light of evening. From the elevated they could see directly into a sea of glowing windows in graffiti-tagged blocks of buildings. They were the very sort of council estates from which Milo had come and he felt at once relaxed and ill, had a racing drunken feeling that he was bringing Navas home to meet his mother, that they would get off the train and see the rise, the tall bank of windows of Canon Green Court. He had a vivid image of Colleen chain-smoking, curled up in the big worn tartan chair with her book and packet of Maryland cookies. For an irrational moment he found himself thinking Navas took after his mother, that she had inherited Colleen's eyes, her intelligence.

Somewhere past Grand Concourse they got out and walked along the gray pockmarked and gum-stained sidewalk, past a barrage of shabby storefronts; street carts of plantains, mangos, and tomatillos; boys walking with their pants slung low.

Navas's stride had changed to a light confident step the minute they got off the train. He watched the irony behind her smile disappear, her eyes soften; when she looked over at him, she seemed younger still.

They passed a fast-food restaurant, a botanica, a pawnshop window filled with rings in scripted gold. Two men in do-rags, one in camouflage pants and plastic sandals, wearing a rosary and blasting Bachata from a chunky radio, were selling perfume out of the trunk of their car. Milo watched the

boys and girls pass, their skin smooth, an easy voluptuous-
ness beneath clothes pulled tight; some were spotty-faced,
some hid behind masks of makeup, some pushed doe-eyed
cherubs in strollers. Boys in tracksuits with gold chains
around their necks, boys with sleeve tattoos, hair cut in neat
lines high on their foreheads, muscles that they'd been
working at.

They walked by a group of old men and women, sitting
in a courtyard at a folding table, listening to the radio, playing cards. One man held a wizened pug on his lap. The street
smelled like fried onions and grilled meat and the smoky
sweetness of roasting nuts. It was a bright, inflated version of
the neighborhood from which Milo had come. Nearly every
shop window advertised the lottery.

The boxing ring was in the basement of a church like the
one in which he'd trained. It smelled of damp and mold, of
sweat and coffee and frankincense. Navas handed Milo a Four
Loko which she had poured into a Gatorade bottle, and they
sat on folding chairs next to a group of cheerful West Indian
boys who smelled like dope, and a man with a cauliflower ear
who nodded at Milo in silent recognition.

Her brother Jorge had tattoos. Not the kind the children
at school had. There was no golden mean, no outline of the
state of Tennessee, no Bettie Page with a whip, like the one
that decorated the pale skin of an English major from New-
ton, Massachusetts, who sat in the front row of his class and
wore thick black-framed glasses. No quote from Charles Bu-
kowski or illustration from a children's book. Jorge's tattoos

took up substantial space on his skin; a photo-real drawing of a baby on his neck, a banner-draped crucifix on his back, dates and initials and the word *family* done in narrow calligraphy down one forearm. And *Salute Me or Shoot Me* on the other.

Girlfriends came up to Navas to sit close and talk, called her *mami*, kissed her, gossiped about people Milo didn't know. She introduced him as "the professor I been tellin' you about" and people eyed him, politely shook his hand. Apart from Jorge's coach and a white-haired woman wearing a house dress, he was the oldest person there.

By the time Jorge stepped into the ring, the drinks had taken hold and Milo watched his tight, broad-shouldered form slip furiously through the air like a ghost of his former body. Jorge had a shaved head and hairless chest. He shared his sister's pretty smile and dark, sensitive eyes. And that's why Milo knew before it happened that the next person to step into that ring would beat the bloody piss out of him. Leaving would have been the decent thing to do, but a sudden visceral curiosity to see Jorge laid out on the mat kept him sitting there, cheering for the man and envying every blow he took.

"You comfortable, Professor?" Navas asked him.

"Yes, thank you," he replied, the sweet liquid humming in his veins as he admired her brother's taut body. "I am indeed."

A light appeared down the track and we formed lines where the first and last passenger cars would stop. When the train pulled in to take us back to Athens, we rushed on. It was so crowded we had to stand on suitcases and packs; ragged fighters trying to push past one another, asking the same questions to the same tired people one after the other: "Do you have a place to stay in Athens?" "Looking for a place to sleep tonight?"

Greek commuters were sitting with their bundles and briefcases, eyeing us with disgust. It was the people from the nearby towns who hated us the most.

I got stuck between a compartment door and a crowd of people and packs that seemed to run the length of the train. It was a horrible car and I pushed around bodies until I was forced to walk on the arms of seats, holding on to the overhead rack. In the next car, I waited behind a couple holding a live chicken until I could get past, then silently handed out leaflets for Olympos and went straight to the bar, where I stood and smoked and stared at the black glass of the window, thinking of Murat and how it would be to talk to him again.

Walking out on to Diligianni Street with him that day from the shade of the station was like walking into a grimy oven. The sun was blinding, reflecting off every whitewashed surface and shimmering shard of metal or plastic or glass on the pavement. Loose papers scuttled along the gutters, kicked up by traffic, the air before us rippling and liquid in the intense heat. Apart from tourists leaving the station, no one was out walking or shopping; there must have been an ozone warning. People leaving the train, once exuberant, looked stunned, sweat already pouring down their faces after one block of walking. I knew that feeling of heat-drenched desolation. They'd come from far away dreaming of philosophers and baklava and Athens looked like a bad B movie about the apocalypse shown on daytime TV.

Murat, though, was smiling. We broke away from the other tourists and runners, headed across the highway, waiting on the median for a chance to cross.

"You been here before," I said.

"Twice," he said. "But I went straight to the islands. Had only a short trip to the Acropolis. I haven't stayed long in Athens before. You feel it here."

"Feel what?" I asked. But he ignored me.

Coming from the white light of the street, we could barely make out the three other people standing in the cool lobby. The air inside smelled like coffee and ouzo and bug repellent.

"Perfect," Murat said.

Our eyes adjusted to the light and for one brief moment I saw how it was actually a tiny pretty place; a modern ruin, an architectural relic from when neighborhood residents were more than prostitutes, dealers, and the transient foreign homeless. The worn marble steps and the tall ornate glass on the French doors. The tiled lobby and tin ceiling; wooden banister snaking elegantly up the long narrow spiral staircase; even the simple square desk where Sterious sat, keys hanging behind him on the wall, seemed right.

Sterious's three pals leaned on the desk peering down at a yo-yo; the string was stuck on one of his thick, knobby fingers, which had turned purple, and one of the men was trying to cut it with a nasty-looking blade; the woman in the slippers was guiding him through it as though his eyesight was poor.

Sterious smiled up at us and turned from them, taking out the ledger, the yo-yo banging on the side of the desk while he wrote. He asked Murat how his trip had been in English, and when Murat answered him in Greek Sterious smiled, said something that made his friends laugh, then took Murat's passport and handed him a key.

He'd booked a bed in a dorm-style cube that had no bathroom; the cheapest option other than the roof. The cool air of the lobby gave way to a dank, sticky, smothering heat as we made our way upstairs. Once inside the room I put his books on the floor and closed the thick balcony curtain to keep out the sun.

"Is there a desk somewhere in this place?" he asked, unfazed by the tight arrangement of bunk beds. He was either used to this kind of life or had no interest in material things at all.

"There's a table and chair on the second floor in a little alcove near the stairs," I said. "And some folding metal chairs on the roof."

"Where do you live?" he asked.

I brushed the sweat-dampened hair off my forehead, tucked it behind my ear. "Upstairs," I said. "When you're done with *The Clouds*, can I borrow it?"

By the time the train arrived back in Athens, it was dark and cool and already night. The platform had been swept but there were stains splattered near the back entrance where drivers came and went. The station lights shined brightly and people gathered with their things, looking lost, runners trying to corral them and lead them away. Drivers milled about, calling to them from the taxi stand, where they could be ferried to real hotels uptown, places with terraces and views and shampoo. Luzani's runners helped people into their shuttle which pulled out into the thick stream of traffic.

We looked mostly for students and the shabbily dressed. Often people arrived not knowing the geography of the city or the difference between hotels; sometimes you could convince a wealthier person that it didn't make sense to take a cab when they could easily walk. They had, after all, been on a train for so long. It would feel good to stretch their legs, to see a little bit of the city, and then lay their heads down somewhere. If they wanted to go out, we could recommend some nice places nearby. There were, of course, no nice places nearby.

I explained the logic of coming straight to Olympos to a skeptical German couple who were fussing with a map; it was dark enough that they wouldn't have a real sense of the disrepair of the place until they walked outside in the morning—and they'd be too tired to leave when they got up to their room tonight. Once I had them, three more tourists agreed to come along with us. Which meant I'd be able to eat a meal tomorrow and drink tonight.

They lined up on the steps looking sweaty and exhausted, hunched beneath their packs. The things they couldn't part with for a few weeks. Pairs of shoes tied together at the laces hung from their shoulders, cameras around their necks, rolled-up straw mats to lie down on because sand or sidewalk wouldn't do, bottles of water, sunglasses, the secret passport, credit card, and money pouch hanging around their necks, visible through the college insignia T-shirts or the fluorescently colored tank tops. They were weighted down. Junk hung all over them. And I knew inside the packs it was worse still, ridiculous amounts of socks and underwear, I was sure. Travel games, Walkmans, souvenirs, bags to carry dirty clothes in, Frisbees, alarm clocks, fifteen shirts, and ten pairs of shorts, not to mention the right clothes for the disco, the hats to keep them from dehydrating too fast, the film, and the plastic film canisters now filled with drugs scored in Amsterdam, the travel guides, Eurail passes, the vitamins, conditioners, shampoos, and soaps, perfumes, toothpaste, sunscreen. Condoms, travel mugs, cassettes, the bags to put new souvenirs, new clothing, and other artifacts in, and of course a memento or two from home. They carried it all, and now they leaned near the door of Olympos, one behind the other, newly exchanged money in hand.

"Do they take our passports?" asked a Danish boy rummaging through the zipper belt at his waist.

I laughed.

"They do," I said.

I slipped behind the line of tourists and ran upstairs to my room to put on the shirt I usually used as a towel and to get a pack of cigarettes, sat on my bed while it spun, staring at my boots, then checked to make sure my own passport was still there, flipped through the pages for a small, square photograph of my uncle that I carried. Dare standing in a field, holding his helmet, his red and white chute still connected, flattened, out of focus in the background, his cheeks flushed and sooty. The sun hits him and the shadow of his lean body marks the ground with a straight black line.

I would call him later when it was morning there, I thought, before he went running. Or maybe when it was night. Or maybe I never would again. I put the picture back and stood up, throwing the wall onto the ceiling, strained to focus my eyes, and thought what a bad idea it had been to go upstairs. I would walk it off on the way to Drinks Time, I thought, stepped out into the hall. My legs had fallen asleep, my hands felt clumsy and numb. I fumbled with the key for what seemed like hours, then finally turned and pounded heavily and blindly down the stairs.

The twisted column of empty space jerked in and out of focus. I hit the reception at last and ran straight into Sterious, who put my commission money into my hand.

"Off to Drinks Time now?" he said.

I nodded.

The chill of night tore through me as I stepped outside. The bank of red lights cast their glow like little blood pools all down the block. And I ran to blur the gaze of men out on the street who might mistake me for someone small and weak.

D are said the fire they'd put out that day had been caused by a car exploding. Someone put a rag into the gas tank and lit it like a wick and the car blew up and trees caught fire and then part of the valley caught fire.

He and some other men put it out and made it home in time to eat dinner. That's a good day.

"Why would someone blow up a car?"

He shook his head, wiped his face. "Eat your food," he said, pointing with his fork at my plate.

It was a placid, sweet-smelling evening. Lightning bugs were out and the windows were open; the song of peepers echoed up from edges of the deep green pond.

I took another bite of venison. We had so much deer in the freezer I could barely remember the taste of anything else. I thought about the swift lean lines of the deers' bodies as I chewed; they were elegant, terrified, about to be hanging upside down from the tree at the back of the drive.

One time, years ago, when Dare and I were playing cards, we stopped to watch a doe grazing by the drainage ditch in front of the house. He took out his handgun and shot it from the living room window and I remember laughing so hard I had to wipe tears from my face.

Dare said, "Go on downstairs and get the tack skinner, we'll get it dressed before it's too dark."

I shook my head. My stomach hurt. "Why don't we wait until civilization actually ends to live like this?" I asked.

"Do it, Bone," he said.

"What makes you think we will ever need that much deer meat?" I asked.

"Forty-five thousand Russian nuclear warheads," he said. "And all the ones pointing right back at them."

Occasionally we'd eat rabbit or squirrel or pheasant, or some other gamey change. We had dozens of shrink-wrapped packs of dried venison in the basement, too, which I'd occasionally throw out. The idea of spending the end times in an underground bunker playing cards with Dare, surrounded by posters of forests and coastlines, was fine if the outside world was nothing but shadows and fires. But I wasn't going to do it while eating nothing but deer jerky.

"Why would someone blow up a car?" I asked him again.

"There was something in the car they wanted to hide," he said, getting up and going to the sink. He would come home thirsty, sometimes drank a whole gallon of water in several long gulps. He'd shower at the base but his skin still looked raw. He scratched and rubbed his hands over the indentations the helmet left on his forehead.

"What did they want to hide?"

He shrugged and his eyes looked blank and wet. "Dunno specifically," he said, but I could tell by his face that he did know specifically; it was the same look he had when he picked me up from my old house. Whatever it was that Dare had seen, he felt bad about it for me and tired for himself.

"Dunno," he said again. "They did a real good job of it, though."

After I'd cleared the table and washed the dishes, we went outside to sit on the front porch and watch the sky get darker. Dare tipped his folding chair back so it touched the metal siding on the house.

"How was school?" he asked.

"Good," I said, as though I'd actually gone.

When Dare was at work I ran to the Okanogan County Library and lay in the stacks reading. I had no plans to keep attending Liberty Bell Junior High.

"I want to blow up a car," I told him.

He looked up and the corner of his mouth twitched.

"Just don't do it anywhere near the woods," he said.

D rinks Time played old American movies on a large-screen TV, and the place was filled with runners spending the night in a stupefied nostalgia, drunk on ouzo and Amstel, our feet sticking to the grimy floor.

Candy and Stephan were talking about the fight; Stephan was bruised and swollen and sick-looking. Candy said Tom was to blame and got what he deserved. And most people said "If it wasn't for Declan" or "Thank god for Declan." Then someone began singing the IRA song *Come out you black and tans come out and fight me like a man* as if runners had experienced eight hundred years of oppression by Greek cab drivers, as if Stephan was Bobby Sands.

"Do you want another drink?" Candy asked.

The drinking was not good for forgetting or remembering. The bar was too loud, the movie impossible to watch and the only voices I wanted to hear were Jasper's and Milo's, wanted to go back to the room and find them there.

* * *

I remembered waking up from the sound of traffic and the sudden shock of sobriety and letting myself into the room through the balcony doors. Milo was sleeping in his boxers, hands locked over the pillow on his head. His long, flat feet hung off the edge of the mattress, which was ringed with their possessions. Bottles, cigarettes, clothes, books and comic books, scraps of paper, pens.

Jasper lay unconscious beside him. Tender looking, his pale skin shone in the gray light like a body floating just below the surface of water. I remember being very awake that night and sitting on the cold tile with my back pressed against the wall, smoking his cigarettes and trying to read one of his books by the light of the burning ash. They turned in their sleep, held one another. Jasper breathed heavily and I held the cigarette close to his face so I could see him better in the red glow. Smelled his hair, put my cheek against his.

We'd drifted south from the same lost places to find this life. Bright overcast haze, darkness and clouds, traffic and silence, the smell of diesel and baking bread. And all around the low white postwar architecture and empty plazas and crowded ruins, the temples built by slaves, like an internal landscape at last made visible.

Jasper could sleep but Milo would eventually wake. "Com'ed, why are you up? Come to bed, little Bride."

I would curl beside him, my back to his chest, his hands

along my skin, and we'd doze, the three of us, a tangle of limbs.

Now I had nothing, no letter, no message, not one book left behind.

"I think it was genetic," Candy said, looking down at the condensation on her glass. The sound of the bar suddenly loud all around and I must have asked her a question.

"He probably had some predisposition to dying young, weak liver."

"Who?"

"Who do you bloody think? Last I talked to him, he was headed to Drinks Time from that shite flea market past Monastiraki; had some things to sell, he said. Because he was going back to school in the Alba Cathedral to study nonexistent objects. What? That's what he said. Got quite angry when I laughed. Next time I came round Drinks Time, day or so later, he was gone. That week it got hot. They said his parents came."

"Why does everyone keep saying when it *got* hot? It's always hot."

"Not like this," Candy said. "Your shoes melted to the sidewalk. Bunch a people died that week from the heat. You musta read 'bout it, nah? D'you stop reading the news after Murat?"

I said, "Where's Milo?"

"Who?"

I looked at her incredulously. "*Milo.*"

"Right, your boyfriend's boyfriend. I got no clue, love. Left after a run; didn't meet us back here, either, did he?"

On the television there was a montage of aerial views: cliffs, oceans, forests, highways, buildings, factories. I drank the last of my pint, closed my eyes and the images kept flashing: white deer, men walking through the trees out into a bloom of asphodels. A river creaking as it froze. And tangled in the weeds on the low muddy bank, a tiny paper house on fire.

Milo didn't expect to see Navas in his office at the usual time because he'd seen her barely four hours earlier. She was yelling that she was going to "give a mother-fucker a beat-down" for thinking he was "all that." Apparently he'd thought he was "all that" since back when he got into Horace fucking Mann.

She was yelling this outside the building of the better fighter, who, within nine minutes, had cut her brother Jorge's face, buckled him with a punch to the belly, and dropped him straight down like a pillar of sand. Milo tried to talk her out of climbing the fire escape.

"Shut up, Professor!" She twisted roughly away from his touch. "Nobody even *understands* what the fuck you're *saying* with that white boy accent! Why's your voice even *sound* like that?"

In the end he let her stand on his shoulders so she could grab the metal ladder and pull herself up, then paced below the fire escape smoking while she made out with the kid who'd thumped her brother. He called up to them occasionally to remind her he was there and to ask if they had any Four Loko. There was no more drink, but the fighter said someone named Alexis could give him a ride home, because Alexis was leaving for work in midtown and owned a car. Milo didn't know who Alexis was but waited, as finding the underground seemed too great a task. By the time Alexis came down wearing a suit and tie and carrying a backpack, Navas had gone inside with the winner and it was starting to get light.

Alexis said, "Good morning, Professor."

"Oh," Milo said.

In the car he learned that Alexis was twenty-six years old, had no Four Loko, and hadn't seen the fight. He didn't know if Jorge had a boyfriend but suspected he might have a girlfriend. She was the mother of the baby whose image was tattooed on his neck.

After a sickening drive, which made Milo realize he was no longer drunk but quite hungover and possibly suffering heart palpitations, Alexis dropped him outside the subway at Fifty-Third Street, gave him two dollars for coffee, and said, "Have a blessed day."

Traffic was jammed, the sidewalk thick with people in suits. The scraping, grinding din of a street cleaner was too much. Milo threw up in a garbage can, then made his way downtown.

He was in his office, jittery and raw, still wearing clothes from the day before and aware of some occluded feeling that he might at any minute lose consciousness, when Navas came by. Perfectly put together, happier than usual, and ready to talk about poetry.

Navas was, it was becoming increasingly clear, some kind of god. She sat by the window, lit a cigarette, and sighed out a cloud of smoke, her face breaking into a smile. He wished desperately that they could lie on the floor together and take a nap. The idea of going back into the classroom, of reading poetry by people who'd never held jobs, traveled with their parent's money, and took pictures of themselves all day long was nauseating.

Maybe he would go home and Navas would come with him. If they stopped for a drink, things would be brighter, the sickness would lift. They could head over to Tompkins Square Park and spend some time with the right kind of people.

Navas flicked ashes out onto the ledge. She was so tempered and self-possessed, he thought for a moment the night before hadn't happened and that she might not actually exist but was a phantom he'd created. He sat down and pressed his back against the cool wall, rested his head on the metal of the radiator, covered his eyes with his hand.

Then, as if to confirm his fears that she was a hallucination, Navas said, "*Running* is *Anatomy of the World.*"

Milo reached out and pinched her.

"Ow, what the fuck?" she said, slapping his hand away. "If I'm wrong, tell me; you don't gotta do shit like that. It is, though, right? It's full of anagrams of the John Donne poem."

"Where did you read that?"

"I didn't! I woke up this morning and was, like, the stanzas are paired. You can read them back-to-back; the content's like a reply or a contradiction. *Then* I took some of the words apart and got this: 'She, she is dead, she's dead: when thou know'st this thou know'st how dry a cinder the world is!' In *Running* the gender's changed but—"

"It's not the same poem," Milo said.

"No," she said, "because *Running*'s not a eulogy. It's a confession."

Dare understood about the history of man: the potato famine, the Holocaust, the slave trade, Malthusian disasters, the earth's atmosphere disappearing, rising oceans, nuclear arsenals, government surveillance. After listening to his history lessons, I doubted the stupidity of man could be survived with just a crank radio, a generator, and enough canned food to last a year, but I respected him for trying.

When I was fifteen Dare taught me to hunt with a bow and arrow instead of a gun, and bought me a good skinning knife. In the future he said we couldn't count on getting ammunition.

He taught me to build lean-tos, though we would probably have to stay in the basement because of the radiation. We tanned deer hides, scraping every bit of flesh and fat from inside the skin, then stretching it to dry, sanding it smooth; put the deer's brain in hot water and mashed it, then soaked their hides in the mash to tan the leather; sealed the brain oils in by smoking them over a hole filled with coals. The smell would cling to my clothes, seep into my own skin.

Sometimes he'd sell the hides and give me the money.

I bought fertilizer from the garden shop and peroxide from the drugstore; stole M-80s and sparklers and boxes of matches, plastic containers and bottles, wicks and wires and clocks, nails and glass. I couldn't see how hiding under the house would fix the immediate problem. I'd lie in the stacks at the library, immersed in research. These studies might have remained purely theoretical if Dare hadn't found my toolbox.

"Jesus fucking Christ, Bonehead, what the fuck are you planning on doing with all this shit?"

I shrugged.

"You don't know?" he asked. "You don't know?"

"Blow something up," I said, annoyed because he could clearly see for himself.

"Blow what up?"

I shrugged again. I'd not been able to find a car and put a rag in the gas tank and light it. I couldn't use our car because he needed it to drive to work.

"You can't keep explosive stuff around. You could blow your arm off or worse. You could really hurt someone. God-damn it. How much of this shit do you have? Why the fuck do you do stuff like this, Bridey? Why?"

"I don't know," I said. "I wanted to."

He had a look on his face like he was standing in the bright sun.

"Carlos the Jackal," I said, "would have been more successful if he'd had a better understanding of explosives."

"Why the fuck do you know about Carlos the Jackal?" he was asking himself in a whisper, the same way he would say, "Why won't you comb your hair?"

Dare's face flushed. "Bone," he said calmly, ran his hands over his head and stood staring at the floor for a minute. He looked like he was going to say something, then went downstairs to the basement, came up with two pairs of goggles, and thrust the box of incendiary things into my hands. "C'mon," he said.

We walked through the tall grass out into the clearing by the pond. I was barefoot, wearing running shorts and a pink tank top from Kmart.

"Show me what you know," he said.

I knelt and unscrewed the cap on the metal water bottle full of gasoline, then pushed strips of an old cotton rag into it so they could soak. Once they were saturated I poured the ammonium nitrate into the strips, wound them up, tied them, doused them with more gasoline for good measure, and then jammed them into a wide-mouthed plastic bottle. I had no idea if it would work. Finally I sunk an M-80 into the bottle as a detonator. It was primitive, easier than building model planes. Dare watched me, an expression I didn't recognize on his face: angry, proud, scared, maybe all three. When I was done he took the bottle, lit the fuse, threw it into the pond, then grabbed my hand and ran to the edge of the clearing.

Nothing happened.

I started to move toward the pond but he jerked me back. There was a loud roaring *whump* and hiss and the surface of the pond swelled and burst and shot into a short vertical column that expanded, spraying water and leaves and green slime. The blast cut into us, covered our goggles with algae, soaked our clothes. It was a shocking, terrifying pleasure that sucked the breath from my lungs. For a frozen moment we stood, skin stinging from the cutting force of the water and whatever particulate life it held. The air was still again and a great swell ran back into the pond from the banks. Then slowly the sound of a summer storm pricked our ears, a thick patter of slaps and hollow thuds as bodies of fish and frogs rained down upon us, hitting our heads and backs and arms, landing broken and still in the clearing, dumb like plastic toys, dead before they'd hit the ground. And the pond too— its surface covered with floating fish that had been killed by the force.

"That's what you don't know," he said.

Lately, walking home around dusk, he would look for enclosed construction sites, scaffolding—places that would be easy to break into and hard to see from the street—or he'd head back toward campus to his office or to a study room in the library. Once there, he'd remember about the apartment, alarmed that he had somehow gone back even further in his mind than Athens, to the days when he and Jasper were living out.

Jasper had run out of money when they were near Zagreb on the way to Athens; Milo'd never had any money to begin with. They slept in parks before they found the hotel. Running seemed like the clear solution. They'd save their money, make friends, move on to the islands, head east, head south. But after six months the only thing they'd managed to save were some books.

The first passports they sold were their own, to Boulous, a boy Jasper had flirted with in Drinks Time. He was from a country that used to have a different name, and Jasper began calling him the Rhodesian, though Milo was fairly certain he was from Serbia.

It took three minutes with Boulous, a few hours in the marble halls of their respective consulates getting documents reissued. Shocking how easy it was back then: answer some questions, pretend to be a college kid on a backpacking trip. Fill out a form. Jasper's was reissued within twenty minutes. For Bridey and Milo there was a wait. When they were done, they had enough money to walk away from the heat and desolation of Athens and go anywhere.

"For nationality I put *Drunkard*," Jasper said. They were walking toward the flea market. "And for profession I put *Alcoholist*."

"I got an F in sex," Bridey said.

Down by the Roman agora two men were sitting on folding metal chairs, listening to accordion music coming from a small black radio. Jasper gave them some drachmas though they hadn't asked for money. "That's how they're busking," Jasper explained to Bridey and Milo. "They're not playing music, they're listening to it, and we're paying them for whatever they're thinking about while they listen; we're paying for something we'll never know ever."

They walked for another half mile or so, getting beyond the maze of shops and restaurants to the narrower crowded streets. The sky was deep blue above their heads, and their shadows pooled around them as they passed rows of modern ruins, junk shops, and dingy stalls. The sun beat down upon a lifetime's worth of objects, laid out blunt and bare and disavowed on blankets by the street: lamps and trumpets and old turntables; milk crates full of silverware; sewing machines and nautical instruments, dishes, shoetrees, old telephones, prayer beads, postcards, knives, moldering books in a variety of languages, rusty toys, and dust-encrusted jewelry. Paintings stacked upright against the sides of buildings, a whole section dedicated to the Crucifixion in needlepoint and beadwork. People were selling pipes and plumbing fixtures out of the backs of trucks. There were rows and rows of bicycles and boxes of records, discarded electronic equipment; cords, crates of batteries, irons, old shoes, statues, and Hummels; and clocks and painted canvas reproductions of reproductions. And the whole place teemed with motion and life; music drifting through the alleyway, raised voices. The smell of dust and mold and engine oil baking in the sun. Milo watched Jasper's hands reaching out to touch this domestic wreckage. He'd cut the cast off only a week before and his wrist looked narrow and white, his fingers thin and frail, as he traced the bronze profile of Diana and her bow; the base of a candlestick that was exerting some power over him.

Jasper did away with six hundred quid that day. He bought a Persian rug, which he said he'd put down in the station to make it look nicer, but which he later dragged back to the hotel. He haggled in musty junk shops or beneath makeshift blue tarp awnings over things like buttons, shabby furniture, and photographs of other people's families.

Milo could only think of his mother, could only think he had never in his life held this much money in his pocket.

Coming out of a shop by the Plaka, Jasper handed Bridey a ring which she tossed into the air, then kicked across the street. Milo remembered the hollow sound of it hitting her boot, her satisfied laugh as she turned away from them to light a cigarette.

Past Sokratous Street they found a café to drink Fix Hellas and Amstel. Beside them a happy-hour crush of older Greek men sat, cigarette smoke haloing their heads, eating meat and pickles from small plates, sipping tiny glasses of clear liquor. Milo looked down at the things Jasper'd bought stowed now beneath the table while they drank, knowing if he raised his eyes he would start crying.

Jasper flipped through a shoe box of old postcards he'd found, a collection likely abandoned for decades, that he was thrilled to own. Some were old enough to be in black-and-white: the Parthenon, maps of the Cyclades, sheep on a rocky hillside. The colorful ones were of the ocean, blue-domed mosques, flags, people dancing in a ring. He gazed at each one, smiling, wistful, leaning back in his chair. Then one in particular, murky gray-green and ghostly, made him sit up, as if he recognized it, as if he were watching moving images. It was a dim picture of a garden path, with broken, moss-covered columns ornamented with acanthus leaves, lying half buried in the mud.

Jasper's eyes were dewy and green like the image he admired and they shined fervent and adoring, radiating whatever it was he saw on that square of cardboard.

"This might have been lost to the world if we hadn't dis-covered it," he said. "I'd have easily spent another thousand quid just for this."

Milo looked at the postcard, then down again at the things beneath the table.

Bridey leaned in and put her hand on his before he could close it into a fist.

Now, in New York, Milo would forget he'd enough money to buy coffee or lunch. He didn't take cabs, walked everywhere. People told him the city would be enormous and confusing but it was actually idiotproof and you never get bored wan-dering. The clothes he owned—six shirts, a sports coat, and three pairs of pants—seemed excessive, but from appear-ances his colleagues owned more clothing, had more than one pair of shoes. Milo had never known what people with more than one pair of shoes were trying to prove.

When he went out to Ty's or Nowhere Bar the boys there were so meticulously put together. So aware of their self-documented beauty. You didn't see someone confident enough in their own skin or with their own thoughts to dress like Jasper had; even the punks couldn't. Everyone so *clean*, afraid of dirt or the slightest discomfort. And the conversa-tion was insipid. Everyone wanting to be seen as good—even if they worked for a bloody bank or drug company or built fucking bombs, they had to tell you how they ate cruelty-free meat, did a fun run for charity.

And he did not understand the culture of phones, everyone broadcasting their location to an international network
of advertisers. If you were sitting with a boy and got up to go
to the bar or the jacks, you would not return to see his
thoughtful face in repose but illuminated by the glow of a
little square: anxious, occupied, afraid to be alone, of seconds ticking by unconnected. The maps bothered him the
most. Everyone, it seemed, wanted to know exactly where
they were going, exactly how to get there, exactly what it
would be like so they could trek across a few city blocks with
utter certainty.

It had never been this way with Milo and Jasper. Or even
Milo and Marc, back when Marc had openings in Chelsea
and they'd go out after and get lost, end up fucking in a
stairwell, walking over the Williamsburg Bridge, kissing in
the Remedy, or along the waterfront, or in the Ramble, wandering till dawn.

There'd been no reason for leaving Marc and going back
to Manchester other than the kindness with which the man
had treated him. There'd been no reason to come back to
New York other than the fantasy of running into a cipher
after twenty-five years. He had wanted it to be different.

When he first moved to Manhattan, Milo went out to Ty's
several nights a week with shockingly little success. Navas
tried to help him improve his attitude to make him more of
a catch, then gave up and told him about Grindr. Jasper
would have loved Grindr. It was a list of the exact locations
of people you could rob after fucking.

He had truly wanted it to be different. He had. But being at the New School was becoming a greater strain each day. The hollow, earnest conversations, walking home through a gauntlet of beefy boys who thought the East Village was their campus food court. And the idea that Milo and his colleagues were, by "educating" these people, working for some greater good was just absurd. By late fall it was clear that the only person Milo really spoke with was Navas. That the only people he wanted to drink or spend time with lived at the southwest corner of Tompkins Square Park by the chess tables.

He'd stop at the liquor store after work, sit beneath the cover of tall trees, amid the smell of fall leaves with these friends and watch the rich people who didn't know they were rich go by. There were public restrooms and kids on swings. People watching the hawk hunting squirrels or rats. They'd drink and get together enough change to buy hot dogs from Ray's Candy Store across the street. There were usually four or five of them by evening, people with good stories. A short man who carried chess pieces in a ziplock bag wore a shower curtain as a cape, or hung it with nylon cord between the iron fence and his shopping cart to make a rain shelter. Milo and a woman with infected face piercings and a beaten Chinatown handbag full of clothes, Duane Reade vitamins, and a glass pipe had crowded beneath it with the man once or twice, watched the rain shake the leaves, hit the rose petals, make the rats scurry.

They were smart and funny, especially the woman, but only Steve had the right kind of beauty: a wiry, wily, sullen grace and patient, trusting eyes. His age indiscernible from sleeping out. Milo never passed the park without looking for him.

Weeks ago, when the Christians were giving away food and Chinese women with handcarts were lined up around the block, Steve had asked Milo how much money he thought the recycling ladies made. He meant the Chinese women. They walked from the Lower East Side with clear garbage bags full of cans and bottles they'd scavenged block by block from the bins; some carried two of these big bags tied to either end of a broomstick, balanced across their shoulders. "I don't think it's a very good hustle," Milo had told him. "Not until they raise the recycling deposit."

Steve was opening doors at the bank for tips, asking for money outside the Fine Fare on Avenue C, and selling pigeons he'd caught to a man named Will at Bowery Pigeon and Pet Supplies, just south of Canal, for five dollars each. Two dollars if the pigeon was fucked-up.

Milo and he had gone wandering that day, with their meal from the Christians to the Sixth Street overpass and down along the East River, where they could sit on a bench and look at the bridges. After, they found a church under construction on Seventh Street. There was scaffolding up, the doors were open, and no one was around. The sooty, acrid smell of Steve's body in the cool darkness was intoxicating. His muscles moved beneath his skin, pressed hard and gentle against Milo's chest, his breath on his neck. Steve smiled and his teeth were bad, and he looked away in embarrassment when Milo stroked him, leaned down to taste his neck, his chest. Milo had not felt such clear desire, famished body pressed to famished body, in more than twenty years.

Walking back to Tompkins Square, Steve talked about how he'd been sleeping on Avenue D and Ninth beneath graffiti that said *Jim Joe*. The kids that walked that way to school thought it was his name, so now when he saw them being led through the park by their teacher, some would call out to him "Hi, Jim Joe!"

"It was so sweet," he said. "Y'know?"

"You have kids?" Milo asked him.

"Yeah. In fact, I gotta run, I'm picking them up from violin lessons in Brooklyn Heights. No, man, I don't have any fucking kids."

Once toward morning, very drunk, they were panhandling for a bottle and Milo remembered he could go to a bank machine. It wasn't the first time this had happened but it was the first time when he was with someone else.

"The thing is," Steve said, walking beside him across Grand Street to the Citibank, "or rather not *the* thing but *a* thing you gotta consider . . . what you gotta consider is that you could have a problem with your brain chemistry. Listen, I read about this. If you're not poor—destitute, y'know?— then maybe you're *crazy* to be living like this. It makes sense right? Milo, man, think about it. No one would stay out all night near that fucker Louis if they could just go home."

"I don't know Louis," Milo said, pocketing forty dollars and handing sixty to Steve.

"One with the dog," Steve said, gesturing to his forehead. "Planet tattoos." Then he looked at the cash and sweat broke out on his upper lip. He shoved the money quickly into his pocket while Milo turned away in shame.

"Don't tell anyone from the park you have money," Steve said.

C andy said my name and the silence of the dream broke into voices and music, loud television sounds. Stephan was nudging his pint forward with one finger, prompting me to go get him another, his face more puffy and bruised than it had seemed before. The drivers had done their best work.

"Did you go to the hospital?" I asked.

"He's fine," Candy said. "We got medicine. We got enough for a month." She lit a cigarette, exhaled. "Do you want some?"

"What's it for?"

"Pain."

"No."

The movie was over and now there was music coming from somewhere. I looked at the table beside us and saw runners playing cards with a deck Jasper had bought months ago, the backs ornately inscribed with the word *Ixion* and a man lashed to a wheel with living snakes. Every runner in the place must have taken something from our room, the way we'd been so thoroughly cleaned out.

Stephan tapped his ring against his empty glass. "What are you waiting for?" he asked me.

I pushed my chair back and headed out into the night, flushed and dizzy, then running fast and nearly blind in the narrow back street. My joints felt loose and numb and the lights of the neighborhood streamed past. Omonoia Square was littered and abandoned and the sound of my boots echoed across the plaza. The air was almost cool against my skin. The streetlamps of the empty city drew my shadow along beneath me on the pavement and threw it grotesque and misshapen against the walls of buildings all along the way.

It was dark at Athens Inn, no one at the front desk. I sprinted up to the second floor two stairs at a time, a vicious gnawing feeling burning in my throat; tore down the long hallway to the walk-in linen closet at the back of the building, and wrenched the door open.

A hand shot out and clenched my wrist, jerked me roughly into the dark space and down on to the floor. I lay gasping with the wind knocked out of me and a knee pressed into my chest, a cold knife at my throat.

I tried to breathe so I could tell him who I was, then he snapped on the light, crouched over me, and looked directly into my eyes until he was sure I wouldn't move. The closet was big; floor-to-ceiling shelves lined with sheets and towels made up one wall, and a cot and a table and chair pressed up against the other. He was shirtless, barefoot, wearing a pair of jeans. His tattoos radiated their story of reckless senseless pain between us. He pulled me up and sat me roughly on the chair near the door but still held the knife.

"You bloody fuckwit," he whispered close to my ear. "Just what d'you think you're doin'?"

"Where is he?"

"*Who?*"

"Stop it!" I said.

He smirked and looked me up and down. So invested in death, like a hunter, he could see life wherever it might be hidden. His dark-blue eyes dilated to black as he stood in the shadowed narrow room appraising my body.

He brushed my hair out of my eyes, tucking some tangled strands behind my ear. His own hair was shaggy and touched his shoulders, silver strands through dark auburn.

He picked up the chair with me sitting in it and turned it around so my back was facing him, slammed it down.

The knife was sharp on one side and serrated into arcing waves on the other. He ran his fingers through my hair to undo some knots. "For fuck's sake," he said genially, "has this rat's nest never seen a comb?"

"Been a while since I made it to the beauty parlor," I said.

He let the knife slip so I could feel it. "The mouth on you," he said. "You don't learn."

Then I felt him gently lifting pieces of my hair, a sharp pull against my scalp, heard the blade's whisper and fine dark clumps fell to the floor.

"I know there's something," I said, keeping my voice low

and soothing. "Declan, I know there's something I'm missing. Maybe there's something you're missing too."

"Who are you?" he whispered, his mouth right against my ear.

I didn't answer.

"Who are you now?" More hair than I thought I had fell around me. "Who?" he asked again. "Why did you leave?"

The tip of the blade paused, rested just behind my ear for a moment.

His paranoia was thick in the room, but it would pass. These things go away, they end.

"I was traveling," I said, making my voice easier still, reminding him how it was. "I went to Istanbul. Went to the Galilee."

"Who *are* you?" Declan asked again.

I relaxed my shoulders. "Bridey Sullivan."

"Why is your name Sullivan? So I'll like you? Why did you pick that name?"

"That's my name."

"What's your mother's maiden name?"

"Holleran."

"Where you from?"

"The United States."

"Who am I?" he asked, like I'd forgotten.

"I don't know you," I said.

"What's my name?" he asked.

"You never told me." I closed my eyes.

"What do I look like?"

I said, "I never saw you."

"Where do I live?"

"How could I know? I don't know you."

He pulled my head over the back of the chair, made me look up into his face.

"I don't know you," I said again.

"No," he said. "But you know what I've done."

The person he didn't look up on those mornings while sitting in his office listening to Joy Division was Murat Christensen. Whether out of guilt or fear or self-preservation, he never typed Murat's name.

Milo did not know Murat well, but he had thought about him nearly every day for decades. A Danish Arab kid studying the Greeks, he said he was staying at Olympos for so long because it was halfway between sites he was researching, but Milo got the sense he liked it there; that it was an adventure; one that could seem rugged, staying among the poor, befriending petty thieves, getting to know a gritty part of town. It should have been an adventure with very low stakes. Murat wanted to be with the people, or just wanted to save some money, while he studied. While he rigorously documented a dead world, soberly took notes on the Bacchanal. This, Milo thought, was why Jasper hated him and why ultimately he may have been deserving of hate.

Murat should never have come around that day to give Bridey *The Clouds*.

"Quite a place for scholars up here," he had said in that genial singsong lilt, and the words made Jasper wince. Milo passed Murat the bottle and he sipped, held it out skeptically, gave it back saying "No," then turned to Bridey. "I'm going to Delphi tomorrow, if you'd like to come."

"Making a pilgrimage to the oracle, then?" Jasper said. A new cut on his face, the price of a poorly timed joke, had begun to scab, and he scratched it absently.

"In a sense. Bridey said you had wanted to see Mount Parnassus. Maybe we could all go."

This was the second time he'd asked if they'd like to go to the ruins. The first time they'd had a late night—or a night that hadn't ended and then Jasper said they'd have to get on the bus to do it and soon after that everyone was asleep.

Murat said, "What do you think, Bridey?"

"Oh, it's just Bridey now, is it?" Jasper said. "We don't know how to appreciate these things."

Murat looked at him impassively. Jasper's shirt was sweat stained; he was wearing a pair of cutoff dress pants and filthy tube socks with holes in their blackened toes.

Bridey was already paging through *The Clouds*, ignoring them.

"Maybe you'd like to stay here with us," Jasper said to Murat. "We also inhale vapors and engage in impressive physical feats."

When Murat started to reply, Jasper began whistling.

Murat shut his mouth. Jasper nodded at him, jabbed a finger in his direction, stopped the song long enough to say, "Yeah, that's right."

"Tomorrow's good," Bridey said, not bothering to look up.

"You really should come," Murat said to Jasper. His voice was kind, his expression turned to startled sadness.

Jasper laughed. "Oh, you feel bad for me now?"

Bridey put down the book.

"What th'fuck is all this?" Milo asked.

"He's whistling the Delphic Hymns," Murat said admiringly, but the softness of his expression had gone as fast as it had come. "Apparently he doesn't remember the words."

"Where'd you learn that?" Bridey asked.

"Where *didn't you* learn it?" Jasper asked her.

"I'm leaving at seven in the morning," Murat said. "As much as I'd like to stay here with Pythia and inhale vapors. We can meet in the lobby."

He shut the door behind him, leaving Jasper seething.

"Why does he *do* that?"

"What?" Bridey asked.

Jasper went to the sink, slid the bar of soap over his teeth, rubbed them with a finger, as if he could make himself look more respectable after the fact.

"Use the toothbrush," Milo told him.

"Where *is* the toothbrush?" His lips were white with foam. Bridey picked it up from the edge of the sink and handed it to him. Milo watched Jasper's image in the mirror as he slicked back his hair. Elegant high cheekbones and hollow cheeks, dimples beside his mouth, strong chin, perfect teeth.

Jasper spit into the sink, rinsed his mouth, lit a cigarette.

The air in the room felt tight and Milo took a long pull on the Metaxa. Bridey walked out to the balcony, looked down over the traffic and the roofs of buildings, the light of day changing as the particulate filth and exhaust moved through it. Milo watched her standing there, staring over the haze at the sprawl of low white buildings, terraced awnings. The clock on Larissis station hung in the smoggy middle distance; vast plains of concrete and metal and the constant flow of traffic spread to the horizon.

"We're not enough for her," Jasper said loudly. He began heading for the balcony but Milo pulled him away from the door.

This drifting madness was one thing at home in their room. But out on the street, over at Drinks Time, it became something else. The beating that was coming was obvious hours before it was handed out. This was not the kind of freedom Milo was interested in. Their place was collecting more things. More books, piles of garbage from the flea market, that awful rug. The more Jasper drank, the more visits they got from Declan, the more cuts on Jasper's face.

"Com'ed," Milo said. "Look at me. It's fine. *We're* fine."

Jasper put his school blazer on over his T-shirt, ran a hand through his sweaty hair. Milo pulled him close until there was a small slip of space between them. "What does it matter if they go to Delphi?" Milo asked. "What does it matter? We can all leave tomorrow if we want. We can go right now."

For one crushing instant Milo felt he would do anything so they could all stay together.

"I'm going to push her off the balcony," Jasper said.

"Nah, nah, nah, com'ed. You're not that hot for her and you know it."

"What does he think he is? Some kind of classics scholar?"

"Yeah," Milo said. "That's what he is."

"Then why's he living here?" His words were urgent now.

"Why's *he* here, yeah?" Milo said, uncapping a pint of Fix Hellas. "Why is *he*?"

Jasper took the bottle from him and drank in contrite silence.

"I would leave," he said finally. "I would. But can you think of anywhere that's actually better?"

Milo said these words out loud to himself from the discomfort of his office while he fished in his desk drawer for a pack of cigarettes. Navas came in nearly an hour later, just after he finished searching for Bridey and before he'd started writing.

"In the cold," she said. "On the corner of Seventh and A."

He sat up to face her, give her his attention. "Oh, good, this one's not in dactylic hexameter. Good, good."

"No, psycho! I'm not reciting a poem. That's where I saw you sleeping," she said. "Near some junkie with a pit bull."

"Why do they all have dogs now?" Milo asked her.

"Why you sleeping in the *park*? If it's 'cause I'm staying at your apartment I'll move out."

"Com'ed, Navas, y'racist. You see a black man sleeping in the park an' you assume it's me, like."

"Yeah," she said. "A black man with your face wearing the jacket you're wearing right now. That's not a thing you do in the city, Professor. Someone's gonna come along and fuck your shit right up. Some cop or some drunk investment banker coming home late at night is gonna kill you for fun."

He smiled. "And y've no faith in my abilities to fight, either."

"It is a bad idea to sleep in the park," she enunciated.

"Duly noted, Ms. Navas."

Navas blew smoke out the window, smirked to herself, put on a low, thick voice: "What's up with *The Holy Sonnets*, yo? I think he just puts those things in there 'cause they rhyme."

"You're never going to let that boy live it down, are you?"

"No," she said. "He's a jackass. But I was thinking about *The Holy Sonnets*. Donne's contradictory down to the syllable sometimes; there's so much to pull apart. I do find it harder to read than Spenser, and it's, like, all *sexy*, right?"

"And funnier," Milo said.

"I know. Right? You know, before he became a priest, his brother died in prison of the fucking plague?" she asked.

"Yeah."

"Then why you didn't *tell* any of us that?"

Milo shrugged. "Happened such a long time ago . . ."

This made her laugh.

She looked over at his computer and he watched her read

Bridey's name again. He'd been watching her read over his shoulder all month.

"You going to come to class today?" she asked him.

The last thing in the world he was going to do was stand in that classroom with those people.

"What's Jorge up to?" Milo asked. "He have any fights coming up?"

"You want to at least tell me what we should be reading?" she said. "So I can tell them?"

"You know, if you wanted to stay at your mother's ever, Jorge could stay in my apartment. I mean, if you still aren't getting along."

She looked like she was studying his face to get the description right.

"No," Milo said. "To answer your question, I'm not coming to class. I'm working."

She glanced at the computer screen again. "Who's Bridey Sullivan?" she asked.

I walked back to Olympos as the sky was getting light, an orange glow shining against the quiet buildings.

Dimitri, the overnight receptionist, was at the desk drinking coffee, eating *finikia*, and reading the newspaper. This was the first I'd seen him since returning to the city. His look of disgust was so immediate, I reached up to touch my scraped head, but it seemed the expression was meant for all of me.

"What you're here for?" Dimitri said. "I thought he went to meet you."

"Who?" I said.

He opened a drawer in the reception desk and sifted around in it. "The runner's key is gone. You must have it."

"I don't," I said. "Who was meeting me somewhere?"

He kept eating, didn't answer. Dimitri was younger than Sterious but not by much. In the early morning light his skin looked gray and doughy, and he breathed heavily.

"Milo?" I tried again. "Did you mean Milo?"

The sounds of traffic were picking up outside. He turned a page of the paper.

"Dimitri," I said, "do you know? Did he leave an address?"

He pointed a finger at me and swung it forward twice, as if banishing a dog from the room.

On the top floor I saw my key dangling in the lock, the door open a crack. I pushed it gently and crept inside, shutting it and locking it behind me. Then took off my boots and lay down, thinking of Delphi.

I had waited for Murat in the dark on the cracked granite steps. The early tide of traffic hushed past—glowing head-lights streaking through the dim blue calm of morning. The air was warm and still. He came down in hiking boots, a light backpack. Smiled when he saw me and we headed out, not talking, stopped to buy water and a loaf of bread on the way to the station.

The bus to Delphi was an hour late in leaving. We dozed and woke and saw Athens drift past our window, white-washed, graffitied, people just beginning to come out onto streets and squares. We rode through the industrial outskirts, past factories and warehouses and windowless concrete sprawl. Sunburned yellow hills dotted with olive trees rose in the distance. And then we were on the highway watching the groves and pines slip by. I watched the landscape and Murat flipped through a small field notebook as we rolled through smaller towns and onto a narrow switchback road, climbing precariously into the mountains, the peaks of Mount Parnassus, blue and white and enveloped in an ethereal haze. Down in the hollow yellow valley narrow cedars rose and low broad olive trees spread their branches and the smell of pine was vibrant in the heat of morning.

The bus dropped us off at a newsstand in a tiny town across from an overlook and a modern white hotel built into the side of the mountain.

We sat on the stone wall above the deep valley, ate the loaf of bread, and drank the water, gazing out from the top of the sharp slope at the sea in the distance. Birds were flying below us, diving down into the mist.

When we were done eating, we headed farther up the hill. Sun glared bright on the massive white stones and the gravel paths that snaked through the site. Signs carved in marble at the bottom of each treasury and temple and altar read *Ascent Is Not Allowed.* Numbered and cataloged chunks of columns and massive stone slabs lay side by side all along the way and the place had a haunted crowded emptiness; a long-dead city in the hollow and wooded hillside, the constant flow of tourists passing through, climbing the steps and walking with their cameras inside the ruin to stand before an ivy-covered stone, home to an absent oracle. A ceaseless drift of voyeurs, still traveling from distant cities to walk the stadium steps, to see the field of low golden flowers that now grew there; to walk through an empty theater, the spectator's seats eroded, covered with lichen; to stand before the remaining pillars of Apollo's temple and to be a supplicant of nothing, to dream of the dead and of how beautiful their own cities would look once everyone was gone.

Murat wrote in his notebook. I stood close enough to smell him and it made me think of fire. Not the smell of something burning but the smell of the flame itself, pure, elemental. I loved that he had not found any reason so far to talk about what we were seeing.

The gravel path ended at the stadium and we walked into a wood, heading up a slope tangled with roots and stones. We found a dirt trail blanketed with pine needles and cedar fans, and followed it deeper into the trees. If I'd been alone, I would have missed the entrance to the cave, sheltered as it was by pines and so low to the ground.

The air inside was close and dank and the temperature cool. Murat set his pack on the ground, took out the bottle of water, and drank. Handed it to me.

"This has got to be the place where they talked to muses," I said.

"That's it exactly." He turned, looked as he had on the train that first day. "How did you know that?"

"It's not a secret," I said. "They used knucklebones, prophesy by knucklebones," I said. "It was like gambling. The rich people down there at the oracle. The poor people up here in the cave. You know this."

"How old are you, Bridey?" he asked.

"Seventeen."

"How did you know about the caves and *The Clouds*? Did you come to Greece to study about these things? Were you in school?"

"I came to Greece because I ran out of money," I said.

Everything about Murat radiated a kind of health I'd never known. I took a step closer to him to be near it.

"I knew you would want to see this place," he said.

"You were right."

I walked closer, and when he didn't step back I touched him. Put my arms around him. His breath was impossibly clean, no liquor or smoke, but a kind of mineral bite. When I kissed him he tasted like the smell of stones.

"Let's not do that," he said turning away. The side of his face twitched. I slid my fingers along his body and hooked them into the belt loops of his shorts, pulled him to me. I could conceive of no better spot than this to be alone with him.

"C'mon, Bridey, stop it."

He tried to walk away but I tripped him, and when he staggered forward I shoved him hard and fast to the ground. He got up, kneeling, blood on the heels of his palms where he'd tried to break his fall. I kicked him in the chest, then threw my weight against him.

He said, "Stop it. What are you doing? Stop it."

His eyes were black and he was weaker than I expected, and I could feel his heart racing, feel him getting hard. I pressed my chest to his, crushed my shoulder up into his throat, and listened to him gasping while I undid his belt.

If he had truly meant no, I'd never have been able to knock him down.

I t was the first handwritten scraps of *In the Shadow of Machines* that delivered Milo from a transient life, to the Gothic and Greek revival architecture of a city campus seven miles from the council housing where he'd been raised, and Athens became like a dream he'd had in childhood. He found work on the docks, studied in a building that looked like a temple, spent chill afternoons in stone buildings. And found other people to love. Thrilled by their voices in class, sitting with their backs against the stacks in the library, words rising all around them, or sitting in the pub. He was charmed by what they thought was drinking.

And he loved them in bed in their various forms, too, the boys that would never be Jasper. The women who could never be Bridey; lying on their backs in cheap flats listening to the Pixies on an ancient turntable that friends had picked up off the street and made work. He loved them, up writing all night. Everyone going to be a poet, but for real, not a poet of the Monastiraki metro station. He loved their love of school. Their lack of sadness.

But they didn't know about people like Bridey, wasted and sweaty in the bar of the 309 reading *The Clouds*. They didn't know about people like his mother reading Verlaine in council housing because she'd taught herself French when she'd been sacked and had nothing to do, or monsters like Declan shut up with Seamus Heaney in the evening after killing in the day.

His friends, his professors, thought Milo was an exception, not evidence that a broader, wilder intellectual world existed, and he loved them still, loved drunken nights dancing, loved praise in the classroom; whole rooms full of serious queers talking about death and rights. But he knew none of it was the kind of freedom he'd had with Jasper and Bridey, who never once called themselves a name or believed the things they did with their bodies could mean anything to anyone but them. He was all for the GMFA, or marching or making sure the kiddies had condoms, but when boyfriends at school wanted the sexual philistines to include them in their rituals, to admit they were "just like everyone else" Milo wanted none of it.

"I'm not the least bit like them, am I?" he said. "Don't need a fascist to acknowledge my humanity."

Then the book was published and he was supposed to let the school or the country lay claim to him, and that's when it all came apart.

He spent months crying after the Witter Bynner. Couldn't

get through a conversation. Couldn't hear "Congratulations" or "Well done" or "Fair play to you." Cringed through interviews. The recognition was blinding and blighting, and after the award he became a blank to himself unless he was writing; thought nothing about Jasper or Bridey for years at a time. But when he put pen to paper they were all that would emerge. Odes to lovers who had believed in his work when he lived on Amstel and handouts. If his current friends had seen him then, they would never have given him a second glance.

The book was out, the loves fleeting, no sense in explaining who he wasn't for another second. There were years of silence and work and more silence. Milo wrote *Running* to find Bridey. He imagined her sleeping in a park, washing her hair in a public bathroom with hand soap, walking the corridors of a train station or airport with one small pack. She'd stop to go through the book racks and then see it: a slim volume that had implausibly made it there. The blatant coded name *Running*, then his name beneath it. That was how he would speak to her. She'd read her initials in the dedication, see the references to Jasper, whose name he hadn't changed, get to the sentence at the end saying he lived in Salford, and she'd come for him.

But that never happened. And when the New School made their offer, he took it. Thought it was a sign that he would go to her instead, go at last to America. And he dreamed that night of Bridey walking toward him, a halo of fire around her dark hair.

I went home and took off my goggles and Dare hosed me down by the gravel drive and already I could tell it was too quiet.

Out in the wet grass the pale exposed bellies of the frogs were drying and growing taut. An indictment. Shining silver beneath the blue sky, their arms flung back and limp. Brown speckled fish were scattered on the swampy bank and near them the soft, wet, lifeless form of a rabbit hit by a flying stone or killed by the blast. I knew I should take it for the fur, but I buried it instead. I wept as I put the fish into the basket and carried them home.

Dare made trout and wild garlic and a salad from things we'd grown. After all the venison we'd been eating, it was light and clean and delicious.

When we sat on the porch, there was no piping song calling up from the pond. No echo of peepers from the hollow. I could see the land as I'd never seen it, shockingly vivid and close. Fireflies glowed, afloat in the dark clearing. The forest rose around us in the distance and the meadow near our house was a tall tangled mass of grasses. I could see my uncle too. His skin weathered, hair shaved nearly to his scalp. His eyes pale and almond shaped. His body solid. Dare was alone except for me, living in a one-story ranch house that sat upon a large underground room at the edge of a flowering hillside in a tiny town with dirt roads. He was strong and kind, had trouble understanding things.

That evening the house materialized around me as if it had long been obscured by a bank of fog. In our living room a sunken plaid couch covered with a wool blanket hunched against the wall in front of a pellet stove. Every room had prints or paintings of the forest and of deer and raccoons and other animals that lived in the woods. There were no pictures of people on the walls—not even pictures of us. There were some threadbare chairs, and a coffee table piled with my books. An oval braided rug covered the kitchen floor; the table was painted pale blue and had a metal top. The pantry was full of shelves, packed with mason jars, canned vegetables, dried beans, braids of garlic. The place had a strong smell I'd never noticed before.

I wandered into my room, shocked that the books I'd brought with me were still there, Dewey decimal system stickers on their spines. I sat, silent on my bed, astonished by the relentless emptiness of forms. Models of airplanes and cars and monsters were sloppily painted and strangely arranged on a dresser made of glossy wood-grain plastic.

The room contained a tyranny of objects: rain boots, sneakers, chin-up bar, a fragile table lamp made from antlers. A
spool of thread and a half-empty drinking glass were particularly disturbing, sitting there on the nightstand like
evidence.

T hink," Jasper said, his voice cool and quiet, "we can take planes instead of stowing on boats. Get farther, travel longer, have more to read. We could live in a house on the islands, a place in Thailand or Prague or wherever, wherever, really."

Milo said no, because they didn't need the money and Jasper couldn't be trusted with it anyway, as he was barely coherent. They could hitchhike away, work wherever they found it. It was inconceivable to him that they now lived in a partly condemned building in the worst part of town, with a five-hundred-quid Persian rug.

"If we can sell even one more . . ." Jasper'd said. "We can leave next time Declan goes off for work somewhere. Make a clean break."

Bridey pointed to the rug, pointed to a pair of candlesticks, to some leather slippers he had bought, then gave him the finger. There was nothing else to say.

Bridey passed the bottle to Milo.

"We just need someone to distract Sterious or that other waster," he said. "That's it. That's all, then we can take them from the desk."

"They're probably in a safe," Milo said.

"You think this rat hole has a *safe?*" he asked.

"For passports or money or something?" Milo said. "Yeah, a little safe."

"Have you seen it?" Jasper asked, taking the bottle.

"No."

"He just shoves them in the desk drawer with everything else," Jasper said.

"If there's a safe, we can blow it up," Bridey said.

Jasper gave her a condescending nod.

"We could," she said, her eyes bright. "It doesn't take much." She went to her bag and retrieved a narrow metal canister of lighter fluid, some firecrackers, black tape, a knife, a ball of fabric or cotton or paper, and something that looked like a sewing kit.

Bridey crouched on the tile floor, the roll of electrical tape around her wrist like a bracelet. She assembled a tight little package, doused it with something that burned their eyes, but smelled nothing like butane, then jammed the firecracker into the center, pushed all this into an empty Amstel bottle, and sealed it with black tape. They followed her as she walked out and down the hall, placed it by the door to the roof, then lit the fuse, and they ran laughing back into the room, shut the door, knelt behind the dresser.

The noise that followed was a thunderous shock, shook the walls and rattled the door in its frame.

When Jasper yanked the door open, the hall was bright and thick with ash. A narrow ribbon of fire licked up the wall and undulated across the floor. Bridey watched the flames gutter, then stepped forward into the swirling dust.

The archway was blown open. The heat of the city already rushing in to fill the space. There was now nothing separating the roof terrace from the hallway. It was pure luck the blast didn't go through the floor and open the ceiling below. Sounds of doors opening, slamming, people running, frightened voices, echoed up the staircase.

"Fuck's sake," Milo said. "Had you not built one of those before?"

She walked over and stamped out the remaining flames. Dust floated in the streams of sunlight filtering in from massive holes in what had minutes before been a solid wall. The concrete and plaster sagged as if waterlogged, then more rubble tumbled to the floor, a sharp ceramic scraping as brick dislodged and slid down the wall. Grainy sand that'd once been mortar and chunks of brick covered the floor.

The fire was burning out—had eaten all the accelerant— but sent black wisps of smoke up into the air.

They stood in the debris with their shirts up over their noses, eyelashes thick with the stinging dust, waiting for the sound of sirens. But there was nothing. No one came.

After some time they heard the plodding echo of a single pair of footsteps on the stairs. Sterious pulled himself up onto the landing and stood in the haze of disintegrated plaster looking out at the newly open view of the low white skyline and sighed.

"Someone should call the police or the fire department," Jasper said as he slipped past Sterious and down the stairs.

"How this wall has come down?" Sterious asked.

"It crumbled," Bridey said.

Sterious squinted. "You are okay?"

Milo took a breath to answer but started crying before he could speak.

Sterious stepped closer to him and Bridey reached out to hold Milo's hand. This didn't make him stop crying. Milo pitied them for not feeling what he felt, covered his face, and sobbed.

"We're okay," Bridey said.

She and Sterious talked about him as if he weren't there. Then they talked about places Sterious had docked when he was young and in the navy. Bridey asked him questions and he seemed to be making up answers. He said something about mermaids. They were laughing.

Jasper returned whistling and carrying a bottle in a paper bag.

"What the fireman said?" Sterious asked.

"About what?" he said. "Oh, right. Nothing, they'll send someone by." He unscrewed the cap on the bottle, handing it first to Sterious. The four of them stood in the center of the hallway drinking Metaxa and looking out at the unobstructed view of the city. The building directly across from the blast was lower than Olympos; they looked down at people on the rooftops, bringing their washing in from the line and staring up at them.

No one else came to see what had happened; no one called the police.

No one cleaned up the larger chunks of debris. Sometimes, Milo thought, if he went back there he would still see their footprints in the dust.

"I tell you this," Sterious said, once the new bottle had gone around. "It's not look so bad."

They could see across to the hills and cranes and ruins. Sterious stretched his palm out flat so it looked like the Temple of Athena was resting upon it. "Who has camera?" He smiled. "I have picture at home of holding up the King Tut's grave too. Also the moon." He pinched his fingers together. "Like a Communion wafer."

Once Sterious shuffled back downstairs, Jasper emptied his pockets. On his way through the lobby he'd checked the front desk. He tossed eight passports onto the bed.

"There was no safe," he said.

On the TV above the bar, a car chase flickered brightly by. After leaving the hotel we had nowhere to be until the 309 but Drinks Time. Milo put his feet up on the table and tipped his chair back. Jasper went up to get more pints, leaving the passports facedown on the table like cards in a memory game.

"Truly, we can't be the only people doing this," Jasper said when he returned, setting the glasses out in front of us. "What about Dieter the witch-boy? How does he have money to travel or buy his pointy magic shoes or whatever?"

"Is that a real person?"

"Where?" Jasper turned around.

"No," I said. "Dieter the boy-witch."

"*Witch*-boy," he said. "He's real, Bridey. You should pay more attention. That German waster with the knuckle tattoos. I don't like him very much at all. Always trying to be helpful and keeps telling us about moving to Amsterdam or

Berlin to *do* something. He wants to *do* something about how *they* are always telling us what to *do*. Wants to go to Berlin and put up a banner outside an empty building or something. Utter moron."

"I don't even know who that is," Milo said, then muttered "Witch-boy" to himself.

"Well, it's probably because he cast a spell on you so you can't remember." Jasper lit a cigarette. "But I am *not* going to go live in Berlin, and no one is telling us what to *do*. I told him as much." He took a long drink from his pint. "I said *no one is telling us what to do* and he said there's all these rules about living or this and that. And I said you know that *rules* have an implicit intelligence test attached to them, right? If you *follow* them, you *fail*."

"You think there are no rules?" Milo asked.

"Bridey," Jasper said, "are there rules?"

"For what?" I asked, annoyed that he'd given me an empty pint.

"But you and Dieter think the same thing," Milo said.

"Darling," Jasper said, "do you really think someone with mystical symbols tattooed on his knuckles doesn't believe in rules?"

"Why do I have this empty glass?" I asked.

"You've finished it," Milo said. "And it's your round."

Jasper was opening each document. They seemed like toys, like monopoly money. All the stamps and stickers, these IDs that defined you as a citizen of a made-up place men claimed by repeatedly pouring blood all over the ground.

When I brought back the next three pints, Jasper had separated the passports into piles.

"Dunno if these are good to have or not," he said. "Some places won't let you in if you've got a stamp from Israel—but there's certainly people who'd want to get their hands on one.

"Oh, hel-lo," he said interrupting himself. He held up a red passport with gold lettering, turned it sideways, handed it to Milo.

"We can't sell that," Milo said.

"Of course we can," Jasper said. "Bet we can get a thousand quid for it."

"We shouldn't do it 's' what I mean."

"Of course we should," Jasper said, his voice growing malign. "It has a picture of an Arab on it, from a lovely socialist democracy, no travel restrictions, stamps from far and wide. It's the best one in the pile."

I pulled it from his hand. "No way, man. What's he gonna do?"

"Why do you care? Since your pilgrimage to the oracle you haven't said one word to him."

Milo said, "All he's got to do—right?—is go to the consulate like everyone else, say it was stolen . . . which isn't a lie."

"I thought you were against it," I said.

"I am," he said.

I said, "We've already spent fifteen hundred dollars on drinking and on junk from the flea market which *he* has hoarded, destroyed, or given away."

"It was a mistake to have bought that bale of copper wire," Jasper said.

He lit a cigarette off the one he'd finished. I could see the long, thin scar by his jaw. I could see every bone in his face, sharply defined, when he turned his head.

Murat's passport brought in the most money. Two others earned four hundred quid each. The rest Jasper kept, said he would sell them when they got to wherever they were going.

As before, Milo sent his share to his mother, this time with a letter.

Colleen was not the kind to question where he was or how he was getting by, maybe for her own peace of mind. The only time she came to one of his matches she became so enraged at the other boy, he thought she might duck under the rope. Afterwards she stood beside Milo's trainer, pushed the ringside doctor out of the way, held the icy eye iron to his face herself to press the swelling down.

She wasn't so much older than him, Colleen. And once he'd left school they were more like flatmates than before. People liked to point to it and say this is what a broken home is. No discipline. No authority. Milo knew the only authority growing up was your own mind; he knew Colleen's confidence in his thinking and in hers. He knew Colleen loved him and he knew being stupid was a sin. She just hated stupid people so much, he'd never let himself be one of them. Living with Colleen, you could be weak, you could be a drunk, you could have any kind of desire. But if you were dumb, there was nothing for it.

She'd read out loud to him at night even when he was fourteen or fifteen, right up until he left home. You'd think she would have wanted him to be a professor—that this path was one she'd set him on—but even that was his business, his accomplishment, the fruits of his labor, not hers. They were responsible for themselves, him and Colleen.

She wrote Milo back from Manchester the summer he was in love with Jasper to say thank you for the letter, told him she'd another factory job, asked what he'd been reading, and said under no circumstances should he send her cash again. The letter started with the words *Dear Lord Darlington*.

He put it in the bag they had packed. A small bundle of their things together like when he and Jasper had first left England. Everything else could stay behind, go to Sterious if he wanted it, get thrown out on the street. There was nothing now that could make him stay.

A low-budget movie shot in an airport was playing on the television at Drinks Time, and everyone was crowding around the bar to get a better look.

I sat down beside Jasper and opened his box of cigarettes. "They used them," he said.

The scene on the television was hazy, black smoke, charred furniture, and shattered glass strewn across the floor. And then, in a corner of the screen, a picture of Murat.

He pushed the bottle of ouzo across the table toward me. Someone turned up the volume; someone else got the remote and changed the channel, flipping through a series of identical images before stopping on a BBC newscast. The bar was packed, not just with drunken runners, but older shabby-looking English people who seemed to have come out of nowhere, their voices poisoning the air around us.

On television a man and a woman sat before an image of the Acropolis. The woman's eyes tracking rapidly left to right.

"Again, authorities have identified the man as Murat Christensen who detonated an explosive device just before boarding, killing himself and seven others, including a ten-year-old child. Sources say had he managed to make it onto the plane he might have killed hundreds." She put her fingers against her ear, said, "From what we've been able to gather for you this morning, Christensen was a Danish national whose mother was Egyptian."

"That's right," the man's voice said while the same picture of Murat took over the screen. "Authorities are still trying to piece together exactly what happened. What we know so far is that Christensen was writing about Minoan culture for university but had also written about the Greek purge of communists in the twentieth century. At this point no group has come forward to claim responsibility for the attack, but some are speculating Christensen could have been part of Islamic Jihad, the group that carried out the 1983 Beirut Barracks bombing. There's also some evidence that Christensen might have been linked to a little-known faction of the Baader-Meinhof Gang."

Jasper laughed, spit his drink.

I crushed out my cigarette in the ashtray. It was time to go.

"This will all blow over," he said. "They can't be serious—Baader-Meinhof?"

Milo came in and pushed through the crowd to our table. He looked sick, eyes swollen.

Jasper pushed the bottle toward him, then went up to the bar for pints.

On the screen above our heads, the same reel showed again. Black smoke. And now pictures of the dead from when they were alive and smiling.

Leaving is what they'll expect," Jasper said, back in their room. "Getting rid of all the things we bought is what they'll expect. The second we try to get on a boat, they'll get us." He passed the bottle to Bridey. Pulled the sheet up to cover his naked chest.

"We have to look like what people think we are," Jasper said.

"Which is what?" Milo asked.

"Drunks or something that live here because we ran away. Nothing more."

"That is what you are," Bridey said.

"Oh? And what are you?" Jasper said.

"Not that," she said.

No one moved to answer the door until they heard Murat's voice.

Milo let him in, and Bridey walked out to the balcony, shutting the glass doors behind her.

"Any news?" Murat asked, the singsong lilt entirely gone from his voice.

"Nothing," Jasper said.

He looked past them, taking in the room. "Quite a place you've got."

"We do what we can," Jasper said.

"You get it all sorted yet?" Milo asked.

"Trying," Murat said. "My mother, thank God, is fine. She—both my parents—saw on the news . . . They thought I was dead—worse. My father's lawyer is suing the network—they'll have to retract their story. There's always a rush to judgment, you know"—he smirked—"for people like us."

Milo nodded. Murat's skin was just a shade lighter than his own, but only one of them had a father with a lawyer.

"Have the police interviewed you?" Jasper asked.

"Yeah, and nearly everyone on the second floor. Many people lost their—had their passports stolen . . . the people in my room and the three rooms next."

Murat took a newly opened bottle of ouzo from Milo and drank. He glanced at the balcony doors, at Bridey's back, then around at more of the things they'd collected. Took in Jasper's school blazer hanging over the back of a chair, the pair of monogrammed leather slippers he had picked up at the flea market.

"It's amazing what you can find digging through the trash," Jasper said.

Murat's eyes lit on the rug for a second too long. "Shocking what people will throw away," he said.

The house, the hillsides, and the forest continued to grow more vivid month by month. The dewy grass beneath my feet was so lush, I could feel it driving up through the core of my body with each step, jabbing long and ticklish into my throat. The rain slapping against the house poured down the gutters and soaked my clothing, plastered my hair to my neck and face. I ran, sweat wicked away in the downpour, leaving me hot beneath a breathless cold that made gooseflesh of my skin. The smell of pine and ozone and rich loamy soil was thick all around, rain clattering on the roof, drumming hollow against the wooden porch, pebbling the pond.

The dark sky popped, streaked bright and luminous with an electric vein, a thin white tendril unfurling across the sky. I ran toward the sound of thunder, feet sinking into the muddy pine bed, and I lay in the fullness of the forest gasping, wanting it to fall down around me or burst into flame and swallow me.

When Dare came home I was sitting in my wet clothes on the porch.

"Why'd you kill them?" I asked him again.

He said, "That was on you, Bone. You did it."

"I didn't. I'd never have done anything like that in my life."

"Yeah?" He was unimpressed. "What was the ammonium nitrate for?"

"Not for frogs."

"For what, then?"

"What's the gold for? What's the guns for? What's the grow lights for? What's the motherfucking venison jerky for? What's the saved-up seeds and topographical maps and animal pelts for?"

"For living," he said. "It's for living."

He rummaged through his pile of things looking for a pen, took the cap off with his teeth and wrote something in his notebook. He was shirtless beneath his school blazer. "We've done it," he said, eyes so alert he might have been sober. "There is strictly no way Declan will stay in Athens now with the Jacks everywhere asking questions."

"We're leaving," I said.

"How can you not be happy?"

"Because we killed seven people," Milo said.

"*We* didn't kill anyone," Jasper said. "*We* sold an item. Don't tell me you're one of these people who believes—"

"In cause and effect?" Milo said.

"Darling. Are you killing someone if you sell a diamond? Or buy a cheap pair of shoes? Or if you drive in a bloody *car*? Are you lit'rally killing someone? Please. We didn't make this world. We're making do with its wreckage. If we didn't sell those things, someone else would." He rummaged through his bag for an envelope, folded the paper, stuck it inside, then licked and sealed it. "There have always been squatters in the citadels," he said.

Milo lay on the bed with his face in the pillow and Jasper taunted him. "Taking to your bed, Raskolnikov?" Then Milo, baited, got up and demanded to know how the people in the airport were in any way like the pawnbroker in *Crime and Punishment*. I wasn't going to listen to the rest.

Down on the second floor two junkies and a well-dressed man from Nigeria were listening to a soccer game on a little radio plugged into an extension cord that ran out of a broom closet. They were drinking half pints of milk and eating a jar of jam with a charred spoon they passed back and forth. I walked past and knocked on Murat's door.

He looked surprised to see me.

"Let's go somewhere," I said. "I think you should go somewhere."

"Where?" His voice was hoarse and he turned away, taking a breath before looking at me again.

"Somewhere in the Cyclades. You won't need your passport. Let's go."

He shook his head. "I'm getting the new one reissued. And I've at least another week at Delphi. Give me an address and I'll write you."

"No, don't do that. Come with me. We can go now, today."

"Where?" he asked again. He shrugged with his hands out

and I could see the scabs on his palms from where they hit the floor of the cave. "Why are you suddenly talking to me, Bridey? You haven't said a word to me in weeks. Where are you even going?"

"I don't know. Away. Come with me; it will be fun."

He gave a short laugh, pushed his glasses up on his face. "Are *you* worried about *me* Bridey? No one is out looking for *me*, they're looking for the people who stole my passport. It's being taken care of. Consulate says I'll have the new one in two days."

His faith in people doing what they said they'd do was absurd.

"You should leave," I told him. "Soon."

When he laughed again, I wanted to slap him.

"I've some work to finish and I'm due back at school," he said. He reached for my hand, gave it a little squeeze to make his point.

I said nothing.

"Do you need my help?" he whispered, and stepped into the room, pulling me with him, shutting the door. How was it possible for the world to exist before his eyes and for him to miss it?

I said as plainly as possible, "I don't need your help. I think there are people here who will tell the police you *sold* your passport—not that it was stolen but that you *sold* it along with others that you stole. And you'll either be arrested or thoughtless people will hurt you."

He scratched the back of his neck. "Bridey, I'm not going

to leave Athens because of this. But I will help you leave if you need to."

There was no getting through to him. He saw how we lived, who I was. He wrote about politics, he studied the history of civilization, and still he could stand there in front of me and act like nothing would touch him. Nothing would ever go wrong.

I shook my head.

"I'm not coming, Bride. Here's four thousand drachmas. That's enough to get away from those guys. You don't need to live like this."

I took his money, though my cut from selling his passport was zipped inside my bag. I thought one last time about giving it to him, but knew when they found it on him he'd have even less of a chance.

J asper decided they should walk to Luzani that night, up by the Acropolis where professional runners worked. A farewell to the city. He talked the entire way about how the next job he got would be playing in a piano bar and he needed to practice, so they'd have to go to Luzani or find somewhere else with a piano.

Milo and Bridey had heard about Jasper's piano playing the way they'd heard about the rest of his accomplishments. From him.

No one at Luzani had been telling lies on the train. The hotel lobby was full of tourists checking in; the marble floors were polished reflective and the bar was elegant; fairy lights and shining bottles of liquor.

Jasper drifted through the echoing space ahead of them, the sharp angles of his shoulders visible through his threadbare shirt. He wore the same stained cutoff trousers, remnants of the pants he'd worn the day Milo had met him, and sandals he'd bought on the Plaka. The back of his hair was a rat's nest and he looked like a shipwrecked boy from a children's story. People were drinking from cocktail glasses, sitting at tile-topped tables. They weren't listening to bouzouki, or Greek folk music, but radio songs in English Milo couldn't recognize.

Jasper eased between tables to the front of the room and pulled out the piano bench, scraping it dramatically across the floor. He sat and began playing. The bartender was ignoring it—and the front desk was far enough away, no one had yet to care. Milo watched as those nearby looked for someone who would make him stop.

Finally, a tall well-dressed kid with a goatee, one of the hotel's runners, approached Bridey. "Time to get your boy home, yeah?"

"How d'you suggest we do that?" she said.

The bartender snapped off the stereo. And now there was only the sound of Jasper pounding the keys, his head down, his thin arms moving languidly. It was no sound Milo recognized, discordant and grating and strange. Jasper began to mutter a song, sweat rolling off his forehead. When people shouted for him to stop, he cleared his throat and sat up straight. Then began playing a classical piece so precise, it made Milo feel sick. He had never seen before just how abject Jasper was. Saliva pooled in the bottom of his mouth.

Disgust thickened in his chest as he watched a stillness overtake the room. Tourists giving one another unbelieving looks. Was this a joke? Was he a professional? An actor? Or was this a *real* moment they could savor—the day a homeless boy came in off the street to their hotel and played that music with a skill only money could have bought. You could see it dawning on them that they were having an experience. Some of the more sentimental in the crowd were watching in teary-eyed wonder, getting ready to applaud or opening their wallets. Milo felt he might throw up, might throw Jasper to the floor. Then, as abruptly as he'd started, Jasper stopped, stood on the bench, pulled out his cock, and began pissing on the floor.

Bridey's laugh broke the silence, then a beefy man close to the piano shoved Jasper hard and he landed on his side.

Jasper got to his feet, his shorts falling below his hips, stumbled forward, and swung, punching the man solid in the face. Those who hadn't left when he started pissing gathered for a good view.

The man shoved Jasper again and this time he flew staggering into the piano, knocking his head with a pop, his face instantly streaming with blood.

Bridey stepped between them, helped Jasper up, zipped his pants, tried to wipe the blood off with her hands. Milo got an arm around him and hurried him out, followed by the receptionist and another man in a black silk shirt. Jasper was just drunk, he told them; they were taking him home. They'd stay out. Of course they would.

Down on the street in the cool air Jasper shook himself free, stumbling on ahead. He insisted on buying a fifth of ouzo at a kiosk, and Bridey dumped it on the street. He kept ahead, cursing them as they walked past empty shops, windows bright and full of mannequins wearing lovely clothes. They passed cafés where people sat drinking in low candle-light, headed on to Omonoia Square and narrower, darker streets. Two men fought loudly in a vestibule by an all-night kebab stand on Andromachis Street. Amid a maze of empty storefronts, boarded-up buildings and burned-out streetlamps, they startled a tall balding man in red polyester pants who was pressing a frail-limbed boy up against the back of a car that had four flat tires. When they caught up to Jasper, close to the hotel, he was still talking.

"You didn't believe I could play," he accused them. "I saw your faces. You hated that I could play!" He fumbled to light a cigarette, the flame illuminating a deep cut on his head. He inhaled as though it were a breath of ocean air. "You didn't believe any of it. You didn't believe it even happened." Blood trickled from the wound and down his cheek.

"Course we did, handsome," Milo said. "Keep your voice down."

"How is he even standing?" Bridey asked.

A small lamp casting its glow on the reception desk was the only light on when they reached the lobby, and they didn't see Dimitri until he was up and raging for them to get out; his breathing labored as he came from behind the desk trying to block their way with his squat body. They pushed past him up the stairs, hauling Jasper between them.

In the dim quiet of the ruined hallway they propped Jasper against the doorframe. Their door was open just a crack.

Milo reached in, flicked on the light.

Sitting at the edge of their bed was Declan, waiting. His feet on the bag Milo had packed that morning.

"Hi," Bridey said, as cheerful as if he were a friend. Declan said nothing about Jasper, who was now on his hands and knees in the entryway, crawling toward the rug.

"I know who did it," Declan said.

Bridey sat down beside him on the bed and began unlacing her boots.

"Did what?" Jasper asked thickly.

Milo felt the sweat begin to run down his back.

"Talked to the police," Declan said. "Brought them here to Athens."

"They're here because of the bombing at the airport," Bridey said.

"They're here to find me," Declan said.

Milo leaned over the sink and threw up.

"Police are at the station because of the bombing," Bridey said again, her voice level and unconcerned. "Did you do the bombing?"

Milo stood, raw and unsteady, avoiding his face in the mirror. Jasper made quiet howling sounds from the floor, laughed to himself.

"What happened to that wall out there?" Declan asked.

Milo's body felt lighter. He'd caused his own death and now he had to wait for it. The air in the room went tight. All of the objects around him were suddenly filled with a desperate beauty and meaning; a panicked love of everything washed over him.

Jasper made noises that might have been words.

Bridey sat close to Declan, her shoulder touching his. "Too much acetone," she said. And his eyes went clear and focused.

"The wall," she said. "Acetone peroxide. You can probably still smell it if you try."

"What were you practicing for?" he said.

She shrugged. "Something that'll take more than acetone and an M-80."

He patted her thigh roughly a few times and then stood, looked down at Jasper where he lay unconscious, skeletal.

"Time to do something about that," he said, nudging Jasper's ribs with the tip of his boot.

"He'll be all right," Bridey said.

"Nah," he said. "Not a chance."

The door clicked shut and Milo waited until he heard Declan's footsteps descending the stairs. Bridey was trembling but her face looked as calm and expressionless as before. Listening to something inside herself. She and Jasper were made for each other, Milo thought. Nothing was real to them. She wasn't afraid of Declan. She wasn't afraid of dying. Of anything.

"He's goin' t'come back and kill us," Milo said. "He thinks we brought the police here."

"Because we did," she said.

She had the same look in her eyes as she'd had earlier when Jasper was playing, as she'd had when she wiped the blood from his face.

Bridey found something transcendent in broken men; read them, not for signs of what they might do to her, but as if they were oracles revealing cracks in the barrier between one world and another. Like they carried information she'd dedicated her life to studying. And it was giving her a power Milo never recognized before. She was radiant with it.

Bridey gathered her things in a little book bag and sat on the edge of the bed looking down at Jasper where he lay breathing soundly, his shirt spattered with elegant pinpricks of red, his face streaked with blood and the pale clean lines made by her fingers.

"When he wakes up," she said. "As soon as he wakes up."

Nothing was more lovely than the way Jasper went about eradicating himself, as though he were the heir to some criminal blood, some sick drive to empire, and he'd swallow poison and steal and get on his knees and wear my clothes and take beatings from Declan, bear a broken arm or a slashed face or a knock to the head and still stay right where he was.

He gave us something we couldn't have taken from him if we'd tried. Jasper was the kind of rich boy you could respect. The kind who would kill himself in front of you.

Deep-pink light was beginning to spread itself out along the horizon, making silhouettes of the huddled shapes of buildings. Milo came out to the balcony and put his arms around me, his chest against my back. I turned and held him tight and kissed him soft and deep, the way Jasper kissed us, and felt his warm skin against mine. Drank the kindness in his shining eyes. We knew I would leave them there.

The air was cool and smelled of car exhaust and I rested my forehead on his chin, then slid down and took his cock in my mouth; looking up to see his hard, scarred beauty; belly hairless and tacky with sweat. His strong hands gentle in my hair, pressed against my head, as he pushed in to fill my throat. Then pulled away. When I stood again to kiss him, he guided me back into the room and down onto our bed, his full weight upon me.

Jasper lay unconscious on the floor in the dim room, skin white as ruin. I wrapped my legs around Milo and pulled him into me with my heels, pressing myself tight against him, our hipbones flush and bruising, our bodies slick with sweat, sealed. The sleeping stranger we'd wanted for ourselves breathing vapors at our backs, a spark about to ignite and bloom.

Milo was drunk before the department meeting and had spent half an hour crying. He'd given Navas the keys to his apartment again. There was another fight with her brother about the boxer who'd thumped him, she said, and she'd need to stay for more than a few days this time. Their mother's place was too small, she said, now that Jorge was being such a fucking faggot. No offense. She said if she could stay for a bit and if Milo could get her recommendation written for Brown, she could kick some motherfuckers to the curb where they belonged and do like he did, only better.

The idea of her going to graduate school made him sick. He wiped his eyes and tried to calm his breathing.

"Why am I here?" he asked her, and she handed him the two tallboys of Four Loko she had brought.

"'Cause it's better than working on the docks in your hometown like a loser does," she said, slipping his keys into her pocket. "I'll make dinner."

"Those are the only set."

"I'll make copies," she said. "And when you go to the meeting, don't be all, like, 'I'm an alcoholic who cries a lot so you should prolly fire me.'"

Milo turned away when she said it.

She laughed, tried to touch his arm, but he shrank back and they stood in silence.

When he finally turned to her, he couldn't speak.

She put her arms around him while he sobbed and held her hair.

"Milo," she said and she had never said his name before. "Milo," she whispered into his ear. "Fuck those mother-fuckers. Be lucky if they could cry like you."

I woke up sick in sweat-soaked sheets and barely made it to the sink in time. Judging by the heat, it was already afternoon. Once the dry heaving was over I rinsed off, ran wet hands over what was left of my hair, opened the balcony door to let in the noise, and stood above the smoggy sprawl and roaring highway, shading my eyes and feeling the sun on my skin.

In my bag there was a thousand drachmas left from running—not quite six dollars—and half a pack of cigarettes. I lit one while I organized my things. The haircut was a warning. I didn't need to know what came next.

I locked the room and went downstairs. When Sterious saw me, he put his hands on his head and then on his heart. "What has happened?"

A small gold pot boiled on the burner behind him and the room smelled like coffee and cardamom. His friends had not yet shown up for dominoes, so it couldn't have been too late. I handed him my key.

"Where you are going?" he asked.

"Just for a stroll," I said. "Have to catch the 309 later. Maybe I should run two trains today, huh?"

He pulled out some money from the drawer and handed it to me, then shuffled out of his seat and went to the closet beneath the stairs, brought out an old cap, waited with his arms folded until I put it on my head. He looked so sad, I had to turn away.

"Sit here," he said. "I get us some bread for to have with coffee."

"Thank you," I said. As soon as he had taken off his sweater and headed outside, I opened the closet again to see if there was anything I could use. There were a few backpacks and one small suitcase with luggage tags affixed to it. Nothing good inside. There was a box of tapes labeled in Greek that Jasper had bought at the flea market. I went behind the desk, which was covered with bits of paper, an issue of *Eleftherotypia*, and little drawings Sterious had made of cats and mice and hairy-chested men with their legs chained to bundles of dynamite above captions I couldn't read. The money was locked in a metal box. I looked for the key.

Inside the drawers it smelled of mold. There were some coins, which I pocketed, and a cloudy-green postcard of an overgrown garden path near fallen Corinthian columns.

I turned it over and began trembling and had to sit down.

It was Milo's handwriting and it read:

Bride,
At Alogomandra.
M.

I quickly shoved it into my bag just as Sterious was coming through the door.

He nudged me out of his way, set down a loaf of crusty bread, some butter, a small pot of fig jam, and a bottle of ouzo. Then he poured us two cups of coffee and began flipping over his set of dominoes, skating them along the top of the reception desk with his knobby hands.

"Sterious," I asked him quietly. "Did Milo or Jasper leave anything for me?"

"No."

"Where is Alogomandra?"

"Why you are whispering?" he asked.

"I'm not whispering."

"It's a beach," he said. The coffee had a silky grit to it and tasted medicinal. He spilled some ouzo into our demitasse cups, broke off a piece of crusty bread, buttered it, and pushed it into my hand.

"Where is it?" I asked again.

Small white crumbs were stuck in the stubble on his face. The whites of his eyes looked yellow and cloudy. He waved his hand. "Five, six, seven hours with a boat. Why you want to know?"

I reached for the postcard and he dropped his gaze abruptly and I turned to see Declan walking up the stairs.

"Now, there's a lovely site," he said. "Grampa's getting the paperboy drunk at breakfast."

He took the cap off my head and tossed it to the floor, ran a hand over what was left of my hair. Sterious busied himself with room keys and pretended we hadn't been talking.

"Let's go," Declan said.

The heat of day was beginning to rise, the neighborhood quiet and vacant except for the sounds of traffic. Sun cut through a veil of particulate grime that had risen like a cloud over Diligianni Street and we walked in the direction of the ruins.

"What's the bag for?" Declan asked.

"Going to do some laundry," I told him, and knew he didn't believe it.

"Would think you'd need to get some bigger clothes soon," he said.

"Why's that?" I lit a cigarette; he took it and threw it into the gutter.

In the distance we could see the crush of tourists headed up the incline toward the Acropolis. We walked through the center of the city with its cheery veneer. Vendors called from the stalls that lined the cobbled corridors, selling tiny urns on which even tinier scenes of conquest and love played out. Above them, on a shelf, a battalion of four-inch satyrs stood grinning, their cocks hard. Whole tables of Parthenons, Erechtheions, like miniature sacked cities. Toy temples built by slaves, just like the real ones were.

We walked through the noisy streets in our combat boots until we reached a narrow lane with no cars, a cool corridor of whitewashed buildings that led away from the pedestrian thoroughfare to courtyards with grape trellises, potted fig and olive trees. Bouzouki music played over the faint sound of talk radio. People sat drinking coffee, playing cards. The smell of the neighborhood was overwhelming, the streets rich with the savor of pastry and roasting lamb, of onions and herbs and baking bread.

I had a deep, sharp pain in my stomach; looked around at the café tables to see if anyone had left their dishes. I wanted a plate of meat, a bowl of soup; I wanted mousaka and lamb and tomatoes and feta and olives and dates. I wanted to do nothing but eat.

I could smell Declan too; the linen closet and soap and a dirty metallic underlay like coal and sweat. For a moment I thought I could smell the blood and meat beneath his skin.

We walked through the cobbled passage down to a cool garden patio with sunlit dappled tablecloths and painted blue chairs. Old couples sat together reading and drinking coffee.

Declan ordered lamb and salad and white beans and horta, spanakopita and bread and cheese. When I asked for a beer he told the waiter to make it a bottle of water.

"I'll be going back to Yugoslavia," he said. "After tonight's train."

"Why?"

"More border disputes," he said.

When the food came he took a hunk of meat and spooned the salad and the large white beans onto my plate grateful for the meal, his apology for the night before. I could taste the fire and the fat in the lamb and wanted more.

I didn't want to hear what was coming next: how he was going away to fight for "the people," because the people doing the fighting were the same no matter what side. Cocked, armed, overbuilt, hysterical, lost because of a story they were slow enough to believe.

I first understood who Declan was a week after I'd met him. He talked about beheading a man in Biafra, joked about it standing around, waiting for the train. I felt a rage and disgust and panic that ran so deep I thought I might vomit. Then it was gone and I finished my drink. Fearing Declan was like fearing the air. The only sorrow that remained was that he was still, somehow, a friend.

"Should have given this to you yesterday," he said, and handed me a newspaper clipping. "From the *Guardian*," he said. "If this doesn't shut you up, I can find better ways."

Some grease ran down my chin and I wiped it away with the back of my hand, took another bite of lamb. Then turned the clipping over to see a small picture of Jasper, absurdly clean, eyes bright, hair cut neat; and next to it a small square obituary.

Jasper Lethe, 20, son of Martin Lethe, died in a boating accident off the coast of Crete on August sixth. The cause of death was concussion caused by blunt force trauma when

Lethe was hit by the boom of his boat whilst sailing rough waters. He is survived by his mother Ursa Lethe, sister Trudy, grandparents and numerous cousins.

"Everyone got what they deserved," Declan said. "Leave it alone."

Paul and his colleagues had ignored Milo's swollen eyes. They were kind. And now the freedom and motion of the street was a welcome comfort.

The air was cold, the sky cloudless and dark blue. A sooty bite of tar and fresh dirt and the musty decay of leaves heralded the end of fall. The thrumming melancholic exhaustion that comes from poorly performing a look of attentiveness for hours was subsiding, and with each step away from campus he regained his stride. Part of this was the scale of the city, which was somehow more deeply intimate than anywhere he'd lived. There were always beautiful boys on the street who made him think of Walt Whitman and a story he'd heard about a man sleeping with Whitman when he was young, then later with Ginsberg when he was old. An urban legend passed on from a wise old queen, but one that made him smile, as though through loving this man a Gnostic Eucharist was passed from poet to poet across the generations.

He couldn't deny looking for muses on the street.

Milo walked past the Fine Fare store to see if Steve was there, see if he wanted to get a bottle and stroll with him. No luck. He headed east, stopped and ate a falafel, sitting on a bench outside St. Mark's Church, watched some junkies fall in slow motion, lovely, the tension between gravity and human force, graceful as though it were choreographed. He walked to the liquor store and bought a fifth to elevate him further, taking the first few sips on the sidewalk just outside the door.

There was beauty in wandering, in having nowhere to call home. He had not felt this kind of dislocated freedom since Athens.

Milo thought of heading to the West Village to Boots & Saddle but started down to the Lower East Side instead. Not just because boys spend too much time looking into their phones, but because he had made himself unpopular there some months ago by saying things are worse than they've ever been. "We lost by winning," he said. The new drag was putting on the most accurate imitation of 1950s breeders: having babies, sharing bank accounts, and wearing rings; how sad it was, after people had to die, had to lay down their fucking lives—this is how we honor them? By clamoring to be let inside? To be sanctioned by the state? To assimilate? And the only reason you are let in at all is because someone realized your money was as good as theirs. Their hatred was a compliment you should have taken. This is cultural annihilation.

The boy he'd wanted to go home with was not impressed, something Milo only realized after the boy said, "Oh my Lord, how do we shut this silly bitch up?" and demanded the bartender stop serving him. "What the fuck are you even talking about?" the boy had said. "What the fuck is your problem?"

When people looked at Milo they assumed he'd been there for the plague, that he was a survivor; but he was not in fact one who could feel New York resonating with absences. He'd known it only through Marc. Marc was the one who saw Alphabet City on fire; Marc watched his friends die. It wasn't until Milo left Athens and went back to Manchester that he knew people who died of AIDS.

Milo didn't survive the plague, he dodged it. And what people recognized in him was a different kind of strength and grief. The things that held people down had no more weight for him. He'd no fear of losing, or being poor or ugly or alone. No fear of being fired or mocked or doing wrong. Milo didn't just know how long he could go without respect; he knew how long he could go without food. If there came a time when the straight white world accepted him, welcomed him, celebrated him, everything about who he was would be wrong. Milo would rather stay on the street.

When he got home at seven, Navas and the boxer were sitting on the floor of his living room drinking beer and eating sesame noodles and soft-boiled eggs.

"Navas," he said, nodding at her politely. "Boyfriend of Navas." The boy stood up, said some unintelligible word, and shook Milo's hand. He was strong, better put together than

Jorge. They shouldn't have matched those two. Milo could see why she liked him. He was clearly smart.

They'd saved him a plate, but there were only two forks, so he sat cross-legged on the floor, drank, waited until Navas was done eating, and used hers.

The apartment seemed spare with other people in it.

There was a mattress on the floor and books stacked in piles, and a closet for his five shirts. The living room had nothing in it, and the kitchen was a little galley with pots and pans that had been left there and a refrigerator full of green things he bought at sidewalk stalls in Chinatown.

"Did they fire you?" she asked after her boxer had left.

He shook his head. "What's this about needing a recommendation?"

"I've got enough work for a collection."

"Then send it out; don't waste your time in school."

"Who are you, telling me not to go to school? Look at you."

Milo stretched his arms out to his sides, his head back. "Look at me," he said.

"I was thinking about it on the way home. Soon's you get into one of those places, yeah? You become their little darling, don't you? Then their translator: you get to speak for every girl with brown skin. But you'll feel their envy all the time. That gnawing feeling they have, knowing they couldn't get where they got without all their money, all their centuries of money, but you could, you did."

"I am not taking your advice," she said. "You are sleeping in the park, you are trying to lose your job."

"That's exactly why you *should* take my advice."

"And you are not writing," she said, her accent deepening. "No. I want the fuck out of here. You're the one who's jealous. You know I'm good, maybe better than you."

"No maybe about it," he said. "Far better than I was at your age."

"Then what the *fuck?*" She actually stamped her foot. "I don't come to your office asking about pseudo-Pindaric odes because my mommy and the dudes hanging outside my building like Coleridge better than Wordsworth. Where else I'm going to study it?"

"Here," he said. "We can do it right here."

That stopped her dead. Softened her eyes. "You want me to be like Colleen."

The way she invoked his mother's name out of nowhere turned something fast and terrifying inside of him. He'd no memory of telling her anything about Colleen. He couldn't breathe.

"I'll get away on scholarship, like her. I'll be the brightest star, then end up back in fucking Soundview? There's not even any factory work where *I* come from."

He walked into the bedroom to get away from the things she was saying—sat and took his shoes off—but she followed him, stood in the doorway.

"Why would you have to go back to the projects?" he said finally. "I mean, you could study here. Stay downtown, with me."

"Oh, I see *you* want to be like Colleen, then," she said, his mother's name in her mouth again. "And I'm supposed to stay inside and not get hurt. How well did that work for you?"

What could he have told her about himself? Why did she know these things?

"None of it worked for me," he said.

"Liar," she said. "You got out and all of it worked. You left and went away and now you have money in the bank. You have books on the shelf. People want to talk with you about words and ideas. You don't want that for me?"

"I do. It's all I want for you."

"You gonna write the recommendation or not?"

"Com'ed, Navas, you're taking the piss. You can't be wanting two more years of classes with people like 'panda-keychain' and 'twitter-abortion.'"

"They won't be there."

"They will. They certainly will. And they'll be there after you graduate too. At every job, at every reading and every interview."

"I am going to fucking bury them once I get out of here. Serious, Professor. I'm serious, now, Milo. Why are you *like* this?"

He couldn't talk about it. Couldn't stand to think of her believing that school would save her, and couldn't stand to deprive her of something she wanted.

"Is there more Four Loko?" he asked.

She laughed unexpectedly. Her whole angry countenance gone in seconds, her pretty mouth open wide, her eyes shining. She looked like a baby; she could have been his baby.

"Not joking," he said.

"I got one more case I can get us."

"Fine, then. I shall be happy to write a letter for you. I imagine it'll feel good to turn them down once you get in, and then we can see about where to send your manuscript."

"Thank you."

"However it works out," he told her, "no matter what you decide, you're welcome to stay for as long as you want, as long as you need. Till the end of semester at the least."

She nodded, pressed her lips together.

"We're going to need some furniture," she said.

Once Declan was out of sight, I crumpled the obituary, threw it into the street, ground it into nothing with the heel of my boot, and kept walking.

Past the cathedral near Mitropoleos, I saw a barber's red and blue sign and ducked down the short flight of stone steps into a basement shop where it was cool and smelled medicinal and thick with cologne.

I paid half the money Sterious had given me to a man who ran electric clippers over my head, removing the uneven patches that remained and leaving me with a quarter inch of hair. He dusted my neck with a little soft brush and I tried to ask where Alogomandra was, but nothing I said sounded like words to him.

I went into a tourist shop to pocket a box of cigarettes and look at a map of the islands. If it was a beach like Sterious said, it wasn't listed. I stood for a time outside the shop watching people walk by in their clean clothes, cameras hanging around their necks. I walked to a travel bureau on Syntagma and asked a woman my age where Alogomandra beach was.

Her face brightened. "Ah! It's, em . . . not a beach . . . It's underwater. A *cave*," she said.

I laughed sharply and it startled her. It seemed likely it was a place Milo was just dreaming about. A setting, not a destination.

I held out the map and she pointed to a small crescent-shaped island at the edge. "Here," she said. "It is right . . . it's here. I can sell you ferry ticket."

Sterious's cash was too thin to buy one. I thanked her and ran out onto the flat marble steps of the plaza, squinting beneath the sun and the reflective glare from the bank of high white modern hotels that spanned King George Street. I walked quickly by the central fountain, past people in suits holding briefcases, wearing aviator glasses.

Tourists in baseball hats, with packs and maps, meandered toward the national gardens or Parliament or to watch the stiff-legged guards in white tights and skirts, like clowns with bayonets, red pom-poms on their shoes. People poured out of the subway entrances into the light and heat and headed across the concrete expanse toward the temples, which were bleached like bones beneath the sun.

Milo had found the house-sit immediately after the passport sale to Boulous. He'd dreamt of this from the first days they'd arrived in Athens—getting out of the city, finding a remote place by the sea, no more running.

A woman named Zenaida said it was his if he could get there. He doubted she'd let him stay in the house once she saw him, but it didn't matter at that point. If she turned him away he would sleep on the beach.

Murat was picked up by the police the afternoon Bridey left. Jasper had stopped drinking, which was not the relief Milo thought it would be.

The news did have to make a correction, like Murat had said they would. But it was to explain that the terrorist Murat Christensen was alive, had "set up residence" in a squalid hotel; that he had aided an extremist group based in Germany and Yemen so they could carry out a bombing he helped plan. An anonymous English tourist had ID'd him.

The fact that no one would use his own passport to commit a crime was irrelevant. It made for good narrative: a student and researcher of Mycenaean culture who was a fool or a radical or a communist or a fundamentalist, didn't matter which. He'd been brainwashed or was acting on orders from his religious leader. None of the theories made sense. When Declan left for more mercenary work and no police came for them, it made Milo wonder if Murat actually *was* involved in a plot they didn't know about, and they'd stumbled into it somehow.

In paranoid flashes he started seeing Murat as someone like Declan only smarter, quieter, perfectly disguised. That was how well the television news worked.

With every report on Murat, they showed footage of the neighborhood, the whole fucking wreck of it, and this went a long way toward convicting him. Murat Christensen had fallen far from the sweet boy he had been as an undergraduate. Old yearbook pictures appeared next to pictures of him unshaven, angry, and indignant on the day of his arrest. Diligianni Street was the icing on the cake: the stark empty sidewalks; the prostitutes in doorways, the traffic and garbage and junkies. And Olympos: paint peeling, windows broken. Clothes hung out to dry over balcony railings. Why would a classics scholar from Denmark with middle-class parents be living in a falling-down hovel in that part of town?

"Why *would* a classics scholar be living in this part of town?" Jasper asked. He wasn't wearing his shirt and you could see the pattern of bruises on his chest and stomach from the fall at Luzani, or from something Declan had done. It made Milo sick.

"Because we got him off the fucking train and *brought* him here, just like we did to anybody else who would follow us," Milo said. "You bloody well know why he's here."

"You really want to be important don't you?" Jasper said, cocked his head to the side, smirked. "*Bridey* brought him here actually, there was no 'we' about it. And she's gone now, too, isn't she? And so is Declan, so maybe they all planned it together. Bridey *Sullivan*? Declan *Joyce*? She just happens to be able to make bombs? *Think*, Milo, think. Maybe she was involved in this from the start."

"The start of what? You know exactly what happened, *anonymous English tourist*. You fucking stole his passport and you sold it."

"You want this to be our fault too."

"All of it," Milo said, "is our fault. All of it."

"You're either a narcissist or a Catholic," Jasper said.

Milo shoved him hard against the wall.

"Oh, that's right," Jasper said, his lips just inches from Milo's. "I don't know how I forgot it: you *are* Cath-o-lic." He smirked. "Like Declan."

When he punched the wall beside his head, Jasper didn't flinch.

"Always so violent," Jasper said under his breath. "You and Bridey both. Look at you: you're like Declan. You going to break my arm now?" he said. "Shove me down? You gonna cut me? Hit me? Blow up a building? That's how you all are. I don't understand it for a second. I don't. I would never do anything violent."

Milo laughed and watched a defiant savage contempt flare in Jasper's face.

"Have you seen me do *one* violent thing in all the time we've known each other?" Jasper asked. "In the years we've been together? One violent thing, Milo? You haven't. It's in *you*, not me."

Milo grabbed his face, and he didn't blink or look away. Jasper sober was a terrifying person. The spirit he'd doused himself in daily had been a cure, not an affliction.

"You've no sense of your own purpose," Jasper said. "Not like Bridey. She came here and she left on her own. And we never knew what she was about, did we? Not ever."

"She left because you're not happy with just getting yourself killed," Milo said. "You want to take everybody down."

"Oh, please, you were already down, all of you. You were born down. If you're so concerned, why don't you go to the police and tell them your version of the story? But no, Raskolnikov, you'll stay right here, wondering what to do until they come for you. You won't even spend the money . . . Oh, *wait, that's* right, you *did* spend the money. What happened to it, anyway? Did you give it to the poor?"

Milo slammed him into the wall again, and this time Jasper's eyes brightened and his face flushed; his smell was suddenly everywhere, a marigold bittersweetness and dirt. He buckled forward, his head pressed against Milo's chest, breathing hard, clutching at him to remain standing.

The boat was smaller than I'd hoped for the purpose of getting aboard unseen. I hurried on with a large group of tourists, walked directly to the cars parked in the hull, and slipped beneath a truck, crouched behind one of the wheels. Then waited. An hour after we left port I made my way up the deck stairs, avoiding the dim carpeted interior of the ship.

I could see in through the windows, families and couples, people traveling in small groups, sitting inside the hold, reading or drinking or playing cards and dominoes. On deck, people gathered at metal tables in the late-afternoon sun or stood at the rail to be beaten by the wind. When we reached the open water they put on sweaters and sweatshirts and light jackets and scarves. I stood against the rail gazing out at the blue water rippling with silver light. Cool salty air rushing into my lungs before I could breathe it. When it got colder still I pressed myself against the metal box that held life jackets to block the wind, tried to absorb the heat of the deck and let the sun warm me.

A light breeze trembled against my body, raising a flush of goose bumps that stiffened the hairs on my arms and legs.

After an hour or so I went to the small bar inside the ship and asked for water and a cup of ice. I was hungry again and swallowing something, even ice, made me feel better. I needed to save the little money I had in case Alogomandra was just some place Milo'd read about and decided to write down.

Tourists were eating things they brought in their backpacks or the snacks from the bar, spanakopitas and cheese pies and fried potatoes. Suddenly I was ill, ran to a bathroom just off the top deck, and crouched on my knees vomiting and heaving for what seemed like an hour until I was empty, just a sick animal leaning against a metal door.

Later, outside and clearheaded, I went to the rails and stood shivering to watch the orange sun spread its color across the sea and slip beyond the crest of the horizon until there was nothing in the world but black water and bright stars.

The boat docked at a sleepy port strung with lanterns. It was the end of August and those who disembarked looked more like locals and visitors from nearby islands. The few foreigners walking down the gangway were blond and tall. Small cars and a truck with vegetables painted on the side drove out of the boat's belly and onto the narrow paved road that ran along the coast. The port was full of tall-masted boats bobbing and clanging in their slips.

Across the main road, cobbled streets led up into white-washed terraced houses built into the stone of the high rocky cliffside. Port cafés, a grocery, and a tourist shop were all closed; a disappointment, as part of my plan had been to eat from abandoned terrace plates.

A light wind brought the faint nostalgic scent of something burning. I slung my pack over my shoulder and walked along the coastal road beneath a gleaming moon and stars; followed the shore and could see the empty black of the sea, the surf a thin white line cresting and rolling in.

After some time the road sloped down again and I crossed over a bridge, looking for a sheltered place to sleep along the beach. Suddenly from nowhere I was wishing I had some venison jerky and thinking about Dare. And that I should call him and tell him about the boat or the stars or the ruins, because he'd never been out of Winthrop. I started thinking how there was always dinner when he was home. Always something. And enough food in the house when he was gone. How I always knew I could kill something myself if I needed to. I wondered if there were deer on this island. There would be birds and other small game. We could live here for free, I thought, feeling lighter in my step every second; we could fish. We could eat things we caught.

I followed a footpath flanked by cedar trees, stumbled down toward the sea. At the bottom lay a sandy cove where I pulled off my boots and clothes, got a bar of soap from my bag, and went to the water's edge to bathe. It had been a few months since I'd done more than wash at the sink in my room or in a public bathroom. I waded into the sea and scrubbed my whole body, my scalp, tossed the bar of soap up onto the pile of clothes, then ducked beneath the cool water and swam until salt burned my lips and I felt clean and cold and alive.

Back where the trail met the sand there was a secluded depression beside some tall cedars. I dug a little camp, collected some brush and flotsam and set it on fire, sat naked on my shirt, smoking. My skin warmed, dried from the fire, and I dressed in the only other clothes I owned. Then lay near the flames, in the clear silence and slept.

There have always been squatters in the citadels, Jasper said.

And there have always been soldiers to shoot the face off the Sphinx, who saw the world as a target, one more thing to refine their aim.

He could say this to Navas to answer her questions, to argue about Brown. To go on about it. But he didn't. There are stories and there is fleeting beauty and that is all.

When Navas moved in, he stopped searching Bridey's name. He bought a couch which folded into a bed, bought chairs and a small table. Navas brought over forks and soap, and retrieved the last coveted case of Four Loko from its mysterious location.

She had so much hair he found it everywhere: the bath, the pillow, a strand between pages. She slept in a black tank top, wrote in a blue spiral-bound notebook, like he had, and studied with a hunger he recognized. Books marked, dog-eared, beaten, scraps of paper with four or five sentences on them lying by the couch, or words written on the side of her hand in blue ink, stopping herself mid-conversation, eyes going glassy and bright, pulling out a pen or her phone to make a note.

In the evening Boyfriend of Navas picked her up or stopped by. Boyfriend of Navas was training for the Golden Gloves, treated her well, and though Milo couldn't understand him, he was not an idiot. There were times when his accent was so strange, Milo almost thought it was Mancunian, like he came from Salford, like he grew up around the block; but it was just the linguistic DNA of ghetto neighborhoods blurring into one, Canon Green Court or Soundview. The words were never what he thought they were.

Navas slept outside Milo's bedroom door, some nights curled up with his twenty-year-old American doppelgänger. Navas and Milo would stay up late talking about poetry, then she would go to bed with the boy.

If Milo was in love with her, if he wanted her to himself, if he imagined some kind of life with her, this would have hurt.

The fine stillness of morning broke into my dreams. Tide had rolled in overnight and the sea was now a few feet away. The cove turned out to be a long, curved strip of rocky land interspersed with gleaming beaches. The narrow trail that had seemed hidden and precarious the night before was a well-worn path to the beach. And what I'd thought were shadows in the distance were actually enormous arched stones jutting from the sea, and the jagged edges of a cliff. Out in the distance boats rocked to the faint clang of bells. People, tan and barely dressed, walked along the road above or headed down the path to stake out a good spot on the sand.

I stood and stretched, felt the breeze off the water, then hunched by the trees, vomiting. When it passed I walked into the water and floated faceup, let the silence of the sky fill me.

Later, I dressed and walked across the white sand then up onto the road. The whitewashed blue-domed buildings in the distance were blinding.

Past the bridge there was a market. Stalls lined the cobbled street, one selling fish and sea urchins and oysters, the long tentacles of an octopus draped over the side of the stand. Vendors sold fresh bread and olives, herbs, and cheese. Bushels of vegetables, tomatoes and cucumbers and onions, were set out. I passed by, crushed by the smell of food, a deep, sharp pain in my stomach. Usually I could go days without eating, but things had changed. Sellers called out in Greek not English, smiled, gestured for me to come to them. Though the place was remote and small, it was not what I'd expected. The whole street was filled with people speaking Greek; I heard not one passing word in German or English or French.

At a brightly painted fruit stand a strong, sun-worn woman threw me a fig.

"You eat," she said, patted her belly and pointed to mine. "Eat."

It tasted like sweet earth, its skin tender against my teeth and tongue, the soft pulpy flesh filling my mouth. She watched me, smiling, then handed me another and I bought a small round watermelon with the last of my money, put it in my bag and headed out along the shore.

Sunbathers were wandering down to the beach with their blankets and towels and now finally I saw some foreign tourists among them—no crowds, no drunks, but older people, families, stoic-looking blond-haired couples with guidebooks.

The sun was blazing hot on my skin and scalp and I clambered down the hillside to a little plateau overlooking the beach, then took my knife and sliced into the melon, so taut it nearly burst at the blade's touch. The rind was dappled green, the flesh inside deep pink with small white and black seeds. As soon as I could smell it my mouth began to water. I cut it in half, then quarters and eighths and sixteenths. It was sweet.

When I'd eaten several slices I climbed down to the beach, took off my shirt, and lay in the sun on the beaten edge of the land until it was too hot, then stood and carried the bag of watermelon slices across the beach, zigzagging toward the water's edge, stopping before people on their blankets, asking if they'd like to buy a slice for one hundred drachmas. After I'd sold ten slices, I went back to the fruit stand, bought two more melons. When I'd sold them and made 3,500 drachmas, I put my shirt back on and took the main road to find a café, where I bought a souvlaki and a bottle of water and sat looking out at the ships moored far out in the placid water.

The counterman was in a conversation with a man wearing high rubber boots. I asked where Alogomandra was and they drew a map on the back of my check. Pointed to the pier and slips. "Only by boat," the man in rubber boots said.

"Can you take me there?" I asked. He and the barman exchanged a look.

"There's nothing there. One spot. No roads. Just the cliff houses."

"Do you have a boat? I have a friend there."

"No one will be there," he said. "Because of the fires."

More frogs came and repopulated the site of the killing. Their voices echoed in the darkness outside my window, just as they always had. I could smell pine and the rain-soaked forest understory and all the life inside it. Their peeping voices had a meter like a heartbeat, or like my feet hitting the track when I ran: throbbing and pulsing in the whole hollow valley, like a boy's swollen cock in your hand.

Life was relentless and the illusion of accomplishing something by killing was strong. I knew this even at fifteen. I could see in that moment by the pond why men had cut whole forests, turned mountains into craters. They did it to silence something that doesn't stop, even for a second. I could see why they made monuments, bunkers to be safe from themselves, why they guarded ruins. I had to live beside men, but they had to be men. I could walk away. But they were trapped. Would never be free.

When I told Dare I was leaving, he turned his back and
started organizing the cupboard.

"You're not going anywhere," he said.

"I am."

"You're a tough girl, little Sullivan," he said, trying on a
different voice. "But I've got things taken care of for us."

"I know you do."

He said nothing for a long time, then finally: "I've tried to
be family for you, Bridey."

"You are my family," I said.

But I shouldn't have said it. Because I hated every family
I'd ever seen. I hated every second of every minute in other
people's houses where there was a man and a woman and
children. I especially hated it when they were attending
events at school where there were groups of them all performing their civic duty; I hated their public personas, or
when you saw them on some outing together, taking pictures. I especially hated photographs of families: the mother
and father, the children in front of them like a litter of pup-
pies. Families on television, families in the movies, families
a constant topic on the news, the need to preserve family
values. For my whole childhood the country I lived in was
building nuclear bombs to obliterate the families of the
world. My uncle had built a shelter so that we could live
underground, eating dried meat and hydroponic lettuce
while other families died. I should have been honest and told
Dare that he wasn't family, because that's how I felt. He was

better, like some friendly stranger I could trust, because he had his own life. The saving grace of my parents' deaths was that they were freed from being part of an American family, and through their deaths I was spared and could think clearly.

"I want to see some things," I told him. "See if what I'm reading is right."

"Well, I don't get that. Y'know? Maybe you could just go to fucking school more to figure that out. I don't get that. You're doing all this work and your teachers are saying you're so smart and you're not even showing up, man."

He started to wash the dishes. He told me to take out the garbage.

When I came back in, he was sitting on the couch, watching television.

I sat next to him and knew that if he was like me, he was starting to feel relieved, happy that he could get back to being alone.

"When I'm out there above a fire," he said quietly, his eyes straight ahead, watching the screen, "I feel like I know my place." It was a story that I'd been told enough to recite blind: the concrete operations of stepping into the sky. A hop and slip from the edge of a machine into the wind's force against your weight; the rush of your body and mind doing everything to stay alive and then the illusion of soaring, conquering as you drop into dark clouds; tall trees and hillsides and houses blazing. Knowing as you stop it that it won't stop.

You'll be called to do it again. Sisyphus, Hercules, Dare Holleran, your name hardly matters.

I listened until he was done. And was grateful again that Dare was my uncle, and that I'd only lived with him for four years, and that tomorrow I'd be gone.

How's it I've no problem with your boxer but you get to tell me Steve is a bum."

"Steve." She just said his name and nothing else.

"Yes, right. Steve."

Navas said, "Why can't you date someone from school? What happened to your painter boyfriend?"

"My painter boyfriend from when I was *twenty-six years old*?"

"Oh."

"Yeah. Yeah, it's not really your place, picking who I might have a bit of luck with, is it?"

"You're sleeping with a *homeless* guy," she said. "It's not . . . He's . . . Why doesn't he have his own place?"

"Why don't *you* have your own place?"

That ended it. Then she asked if he was going to class. Told him she'd assigned them *The Tenth Muse Lately Sprung Up in America*.

"Oh, Anne Bradstreet! Fuckin' *brilliant*."

"I know it's fucking brilliant! You can't just tell the class they can do whatever they want, Professor. It doesn't work."

"It works fine—they're reading *The Tenth Muse*."

"'Cause I *told* them to."

"Yes, exactly."

"What would you'd a been like without all those punches to the head?" she said.

"Prettier," Milo said, "if you can believe it."

Navas put her coffee mug in the sink, went into the bathroom. When she came out, her hair was up and she'd put on lipstick. She slid into her boots and zipped them, picked up her backpack, got her jean jacket off the hook in the hall. He loved the way she walked like she would break anything that got in her way.

"F'real," she said. "You coming to class?"

"I am," he lied. "I'll see you there." When she left he went back to the bedroom and opened the laptop and a can of Four Loko. He'd started thinking about what he'd say in the letter for her, but his thoughts drifted back and were soon consumed by the image of Bridey Sullivan's pregnant body illuminated by flames.

I couldn't find a boat to the other side of the island and had slept that afternoon in the shade of a mastic grove beneath low trees that smelled of pine and frankincense, and when I woke the sky was a darkening purple. A light hot wind had picked up, and the smell of smoke and roasting nuts and sage was drifting on the air.

Below the grove, people were walking along the road that hugged the shore, so I collected my things and followed.

Children ran along together barefoot in little packs, brandishing sticks, and the air was charged with anticipation. Adults walked slowly side by side carrying blankets and baskets, passing bottles of clear liquor back and forth. Teenagers tripped along, giddy, hugging one another, singing the same refrain of a song, bursting into laughter. Girls my age with long, dark, ocean-salted hair, boys in crisp jeans and tank tops, muscles pressing out against their skin.

The road ended in low whitewashed steps, lit on either

side with candles in little glass jars. At the bottom was a blue-domed building crowned with a cross, illuminated arched windows cut into walls that were easily three feet thick. The church courtyard was lined with terra-cotta pots full of red flowers, and the terrace strung with strings of tiny white lights. A band was playing, the music high and precise, chords like ringing bells, the bright metallic flutter of mandolin and bouzouki.

Small square tables had been set up, piled with plates of food: kebabs, and olives and bread and fruit. The whole place smelled of roasting lamb and smoke and sea and the woody resinous scent of forest or church. I followed a loose crush of people toward the food, taking a charred kebab and cramming it into my mouth.

Beside the musicians, a group of older people stood, women in long skirts and sandals with graying hair pulled up off their necks, near them young women in capri pants, bellies bare, and men with wet-looking hair, their white shirts open at the chest; they clapped along with the music, then began to dance a simple metered cross step, arms woven together. The men at the ends of the line held white handkerchiefs in their hands, waved them slowly. And then the music grew faster, and the dance more complicated, their heels hitting the ground in unison with a sharp, flat snap, a relentless downbeat, bodies bouncing higher, the crowd yelling "*Opa!*" Drinks passed around, faces flushed, hair coming undone, long and dark and whipping against faces. I ate and watched them. Feeling the mad pull of the music.

Down the coastline dozens had already gathered beside the water. The surf rolled in, cresting beside a tangled mass of driftwood and debris that was surrounded by a crowd. I ate another skewer of lamb, licked the grease from my fingers, sat on the edge of the terrace, and then jumped off, onto the rocky embankment thick with scrub grass and tree seedlings, the sound of waves hushing against the land, the music getting quieter as I walked.

Children ran along the water's edge, throwing sticks and flotsam. Stars now filled the hollow sky. I took off my boots and walked toward the gathering.

When the match dropped I felt a weakening in the pit of my stomach and a wild rushing power rising up from the arches of my feet into my chest. It made me gasp. The wood had been well doused with alcohol and immediately smelled of anise and pine, which I could taste at the back of my throat. Then all the darkened faces came to light, orange and yellow and white, and low awed moans rose in chorus as the fire grew.

A pack of dogs ran along the beach, pawing at something in the wet sand, yapping and tossing their heads.

I moved closer to the crackling fire, listened to it breathe. Candles pushed into the sand lit the camps of people with children setting out blankets, stargazing or sitting crosslegged, talking, eating. Farther down from where we stood below the monastery I could see small fires at the edge of the land, hundreds of flickering lights from candles along the coast, like a border of stars before the empty blackness of the water, shadows gathered around them, illuminated briefly, then blinking into darkness.

A pack of children, maybe seven or eight years old, had built their own blaze by the water and were poking at it with sticks, throwing seaweed and shells into it, but it soon smoked and guttered and died. I watched them as they sent a tiny wiry runner to the main fire, who came back jubilant with a burning torch and hurled it onto the pile. This was starting to flame out as well, so I walked over and sprayed it with lighter fluid, laughing at their happy squeals as the fire shot skyward.

The girls I'd seen on the road were in their bathing suits running from their blankets to the main bonfire; they joined hands and ran in a ring around it, tripping and laughing as they were on the road, their skin shining in the yellow light. They began a mock approximation of the dances in the courtyard. Their shouts of "*Opa!*" sounded sarcastic, ridiculous, but soon they were dancing on the sand, in the same perfect cross steps as above, screaming out a song that might have been a thousand years old.

A dense semicircle of people surrounded the central bonfire, its smoke rising, the warm glow reflected in the black water. Running from the edge of the embankment, two girls leaped over it like deer, followed by a crowd of shirtless men in shorts who jumped, then rushed into the sea screaming. A variety of children and dogs ran howling by, closing in on the flames and then skipping away, kicking up sand.

Everywhere, figures were moving, a confluence of voices becoming one human sound. I looked for Milo's easy gait among the shadowed figures in the crowd. I wandered and listened for words in English, for the sound of his rich voice. The air was cool and the wind was pushing the fire in toward the land, sparks and ash drifting across the beach and up into the dark and glittering sky.

Every two weeks he would go into the main port town, taking the boat and docking it at a public marina, then walking inland half a mile to the bus stop. The roads were close and barren and dusty, and toward the end of summer the wind had begun to pick up. He'd buy things that would keep—bags of rice, jars of beans and tomatoes, and tins of meat, and on market days fresh vegetables. At home he fished off the low dock by the cliffs. In town he drank in the café and played cards or dominoes with whoever was there, sometimes until it closed. Then he'd sleep on the beach and take the boat home the next day.

Milo thought there would be competition for this house-sit, but Zenaida, who owned the place, was gone from late summer until early spring every year, and it was not somewhere most would agree to stay in bad weather. The house was among several built directly into a cliff, all whitewashed, doors the same blue as the sky, the flat roof nothing more than a barren dirt-covered plateau. The place had no back windows or door. Wide zigzagging steps carved into the stone led down into the other rooms of the house, each off the outside terrace. These steps ended at the sea, a weathered boat dock, and an expanse of smooth white rocks, curved like the bellies of giants, massive bodies in repose. Out in the water, this same white stone jutted up like tiny islands, formed arches and bridges, caves that were submerged for half the day.

This is where Milo lived for six months when he was twenty years old.

On the last day of August he went into town, for the bigger market, and docked the boat close to where the festival would be. He'd no intention of going home that night, left the café when it was dark and the streets were abandoned and already smelled of smoke, and headed down to the shore, walking the length of it, toward the blaze of tiny lights, little mounds of flame, and a roaring fire that undulated, far off near the water's edge, throwing sparks like a forge into the black sky.

His Greek had improved enough to have quick conversations with those he passed, to toast and say farewell to Old Man August, but he missed deeper conversations. He sat for a while on a blanket with a couple who spoke English well. They shared a clear sweet liqueur with him that tasted like pine and they talked about how the winds were going to get worse. How these were the last calm days.

Milo asked what would happen next at the festival: Was

there a boat that would be set on fire and set out to sea? Were they to run with torches along the beach? Would they burn someone in effigy? Fire jumpers, they told him and pointed far down below the dome of the monastery, its courtyard decorated with fairy lights.

Packs of dogs ran, silhouetted by the bonfires, and they talked about how the dogs must live. Milo watched while the animals went from blanket to blanket, fed or kicked away snarling.

They looked like regular house dogs, mutts of various sizes but with matted fur and scratched faces, rough, but not skittish like they'd been beaten, or so aggressive they were frightening. Instead they looked savagely intelligent. He left the couple sitting on the blanket and followed the dogs down the beach until they broke off running.

Later he saw them again on the sand, the one in the lead trailing a blanket behind him that had caught fire, the rest of them growling and yipping at his sides.

Near the black water a row of low flames lit the bodies of people dancing. Beautiful boys and men were jumping directly into them, through them, leaping or springing over them—and then straight on into the sea, screaming.

At first glimpse he thought she was a hallucination: her hair gone, body filled out; a womanly apparition of Bridey running toward the fire. In the middle of the blaze she was simply a black outline, and he could see plainly the curve of her belly, the strength and speed of her legs as her clothes caught light. She emerged wearing flames, streaked past into the surf, then disappeared below the black water as if it never happened.

Milo screamed her name into the waves, wading out, searching, half-blind from staring into the bonfire, crying.

Then he saw her stand, walking to shore, wringing out her tattered shirt. He called to her and she turned, ran, began laughing. He picked her up and she was wet and cold from the sea. She wrapped her legs around his waist, her breasts pressed against him, her arms around his neck; kissed his face, pulled back to look at him, her pale eyes sated, her eyebrows singed but not a burn on her skin, which shone gold in the glow of the firelight.

The bonfires were still high along the beach when we'd walked away, hitched a ride over a narrow barren road, then spread ourselves out on the sand near his boat to wait for it to get light. I was still high from running through the fire, untouchable from the double baptism of flame and sea. The wind was blowing and he gave me his shirt to wear, and we dug ourselves a little place to sit. The smell of wood smoke still drifting thickly across the island. His face lovely and calm.

"Did you come straight here from Turkey, like?"

"Athens. I found your note."

"Athens. Who's there?"

"Declan," I said. "Everyone you'd expect. Mike, Stephan, Candy. The usual from Luzani, same people at Drinks Time. Boulous . . . No Murat. No one talking."

He didn't ask about Jasper.

"Murat was arrested," he said.

"While you were there?"

"Yeah," he said. "Nasty blokes in suits wanderin' around outside our room, looking at your missing wall, yeah? Came in to talk t'us and Jasper was on the lash, cross-eyed, like. He'd mostly stopped after you left but musta been hitting it again that day when I wasn't around. They shoulda taken us in for all kinds of things, for more questions, even, but we were such wasters, they didn't. We told them our room was the hotel's storage, and they believed it. Who'd believe anyone traveled with that many books, yeah? Who'd believe we'd bought the rug and those slippers and the beadwork Jesus? We didn't lie about being runners and they didn't care. Showed them our own replacement passports—said we'd been robbed too. They walked Murat out through the lobby and, you know, you musta seen papers. You know."

In the morning light we got into his boat and he rowed us to an abandoned landscape of high cliffs, stone arches. We moored the boat along a weathered wooden dock and walked up three flights of whitewashed steps.

The house was silent. We slept that morning in a cool bedroom with one large shuttered window cut into the thick stone. Lying with my face on his chest, his hand cradling my head, I was exhausted as I'd never been. That day I slept until night, then came into the living room to read and fall asleep again. It was as if a thing that had always been alert—always been awake inside me—had stopped its watch at last; all I could do was lie flat and dream.

When hunger woke me, I was on a low blue couch in

front of a stone fireplace and it was either morning or dusk, judging by the light. An enormous bookshelf took up the entirety of a wall. Milo was sitting across from me on a threadbare chair with a sheepskin thrown over it, the reading lamp beside him casting a glow. The mismatched furniture was all pale blues and smooth butter yellow. There were piles of books on the floor around his chair, one a children's encyclopedia in Greek, a blue spiral-bound notebook open at his feet.

When he came and knelt by the couch, I turned and buried my face in his neck. I could not get enough of his smell, like balsam and dryer sheets and ocean air. There was a new weight to him, a new calmness. His face was lovely and not as gaunt; his misshapen ear, straight nicotine-stained teeth, broad, flat nose. His hair was salt-dusted from swimming and the kindness in his eyes had grown as if it had been fed.

"Ar'ray our kid. Y'missed breakfast and lunch. Again."

Part of a dream came back while he spoke—birds flying in a white-gray sky, buildings by the edge of a crater, the pyrite irises of a frog's eyes.

"You haven't seen the rest of the gaff," Milo said, opening the wooden door and shutters to a warm salt breeze and the sound of birds and waves. Outside, open water, an expanse of air and sky and nothing more. I stood and stretched and walked with him to stand and look down at the white crest of waves moving rhythmically below.

"How did you get this place?" I asked him.

He said, "Don't think memorizing poems won't get you

anywhere. Owner's off teaching in England. This is her family's house from way back. Practically nobody lives on this side of the island."

I tried to imagine anyone who would let a runner looking like Milo did stay in their house. Or maybe I said that out loud.

"She *did* think I was a no-good at first," he said. "She'd lived in Manchester, yeah? Actually *knew* where me neighborhood was. But then we talked and I took out books to show her, like an arrogant fuck, I actually read her one a me own poems! I did, Bridey! She told me the last girl had this job had been singing on the street—busking, like—on the other side of the island. I think this lady might be an angel, Bride, what do you think? Maybe she's an angel and we're dead."

It seemed possible.

"You hungry?" he asked quickly. He rose and I followed him up the outside stairs to the kitchen where dried herbs hung from ceiling rafters and the shelves were well stocked with boxes of crackers and canned food and cereal, jars of tomatoes and peppers and olives and pistachios; bottles of Metaxa and ouzo sat on the shelves. In the refrigerator, Amstel. A bowl of fruit on the table. I peeled an orange, breathed in its fresh bite, then uncapped a beer, sat at the tile-topped table, the last light of day pouring in across the room.

Milo opened a jar of olives and pulled some feta out of the refrigerator, began slicing a tomato. He put these things on little dishes. I ate everything as he set it out and still felt hungry. He opened the refrigerator and took out some lemons, something wrapped in white paper. Inside, the short, thick tentacles of an octopus, dark and mottled, with fleshy circular suckers. He took down a frying pan, poured olive oil into it and lit the burner, crushed garlic, pulled herbs down from where they hung and tossed them in the pan, then dumped in the octopus, squeezing the lemons over it. I'd not eaten sitting at a kitchen table in years. The last time I'd had more than one meal a day was in Winthrop.

"You're going to like this," Milo said.

I came and stood beside him at the stove and smelled the garlic and oregano and thyme, the fresh briny smell of the octopus. He cut a little piece as it cooked and put it in my mouth, the flavor so bright I had to shut my eyes.

When he finished cooking, he brought it all to the table and we ate and drank Amstel and listened to the quiet sound of the waves. The food was savory and rich and delicious.

After, we sat lazily, picking at the olives. A salt breeze drifting up from the blue below.

"I couldn't bring him here, Bride," Milo said.

"Or anywhere," I agreed.

Milo called Jasper's parents from a bank of telephones on Victor Hugo Street. Talked long enough to tell his mother where they were and that Jasper was unwell. When they came they did not look at Milo, would not speak to him. Would not take his help in getting Jasper downstairs and into a cab.

The horror of having desired that boy could still keep him up nights; the hollow awful feeling of watching Jasper's face, fascinated by the news footage. He'd seen the debris, the filth of remains, but couldn't feel what it had done to flesh; he could barely feel his own pain let alone that of others. The shame of how deeply Milo had loved and despised him was only beginning in those days on the island.

"Do you need to see a doctor?" Milo asked.

Bridey looked up, startled. "For what?"

"'For what,'" Milo said back to her. "We gonna never talk about it? How far along are you?"

She held up one of his blue spiral-bound notebooks. "A few pages in. It's really good."

"Com'ed, stop it, Bridey."

She was silent. The wind was moaning again and waves crashed up the side of the cliff, breaking and spraying. She went back to reading his work.

When she finally spoke she said, "What are we going to do about Murat?"

I turned eighteen on that island. And felt through the skin of my belly the pressing and turning of another body, the quick silent tap of a knee or elbow or head or foot. And I laid my hand there so we could feel each other.

I stayed with Milo for four months. Reading. Eating. Lying beside him at night. In the beginning we walked along the cliffside and down to the beach. Swam in the sea, tasting salt, lying in the bright sun, warm and painless, like being drunk. Like never having to sober up, never having to speak. We were quieter still in the evening. Unconscious for ten or twelve hours at a time, slept on clean sheets in a real bed, often without dreaming. And in the morning, birds were singing and gulls crying, and no clanging from the harbor carried up to the windows.

Summer dresses hung in the closet of the room in which we slept. Short-sleeved shirts with buttons, skirts. I tried them on, slid them over my round body. Most days I wore a white cotton slip I'd found hanging in the bathroom and Milo's Joy Division shirt. My hair had grown in, dark and wavy. I sat out on the deck reading books Milo'd brought, eating olives.

His body had changed too. His facial hair coarser. His back and chest broader, the flesh beneath his skin more voluptuous. We turned and held one another in the soft bed at night. The smell of our breath and bodies becoming one scent. We would wake and talk and kiss and then sleep again.

"We'da been fine," Milo said one night, head on the pillow, staring at the ceiling. "But he'd this whole other idea of making money didn't he? Just like alla them. Wasters in their navy blue blazers. It's never enough for them."

I said, "We all sold the passports. It wasn't just Jasper. He never planned to make it more than that."

"You know he did."

The wind had picked up outside, its force pressing against the shutters, rattling the small boats down by the dock. I got up and sat in the bedside chair, turned on the light.

"Murat prob'ly'd no idea at first it was us that sold his papers. Thought we were just some perverts who drank too much. Then he'd come up and seen all the shite Jasper'd bought at the flea market, saw our place. Once you left—he was hours from turning us in, I swear."

I shook my head.

"Yeah," he said. "He was. An' Jasper understood the value of that kid's story; Murat spoke Greek, he spoke Danish, English, Arabic, German. All Jasper had to say to the police was those passports disappeared an' the explosion happened just after Murat got there. Which was true. No, com'ed, listen to me."

"Is that what he did?"

"I've no idea what he did. But that's what makes sense, yeah? And after all that he still planned on selling more."

"There were no more."

Milo threw the covers off, strode naked to the dresser; he pulled out three passports. American, English, German, dropped them into my hands.

"Of course there were," he said. "You knew there were."

Who else could it have been? That time before she left. All those times with Jasper, when he wanted her there but didn't want her. This was Milo's baby. She wouldn't have looked for him otherwise. She wouldn't be there. She wouldn't smell so good to him, wouldn't be sleeping in bed with him every night, if it wasn't his.

He said, "Thinking again of going back to Manchester, yeah? See me ma, just for a bit."

Bridey stood in the shallow waves, shells cupped in an upturned hand. "Why?" she said.

"It's on my mind. You'd like Colleen. You'd get along."

She'd need to be somewhere for a while once the baby was born. He could get a job.

Bridey walked out into the waves, hair whipping against her face in the wind.

"You could come with me and stay for a while," he called.

She walked out farther. Slipped beneath the next cold blue crest and swam.

Milo was a person whose future you could see clearly. Milo had looked for the house-sit. He planned. He wrote every day, he studied. He saw the world as it was and wanted no part of the ugliness, so he wrote or drank, or wandered until it was pretty. Nothing else suited him.

Murat's papers and a journal were in the drawer where Milo'd kept the passports, along with several thousand drachmas he must have stolen before the police had come. He must have been afraid we'd be mentioned in them, and we were. I couldn't read the Danish but I could read our names, and Declan's.

I left before he woke, in one of the neighbors' boats, so he wouldn't be stranded. It was cold and windy and there was a light rain. The sky was glowing pink and orange when I shut the wooden door of the cliff house. It took hours to row to the harbor, sticking close to the coast. I used his money for food and a ferry ticket. Sat in the hold this time, rocked and slept above the roiling sea.

I loved Milo Rollock, and I loved leaving him where he was, lying beside his notebook, alone.

A boy with a Rottweiler told him they took the scaffolding down on Ninth Street and Steve had been sleeping down by Hamilton Fish Park across Houston. He went there but couldn't find him, drank the bottle himself.

Navas would be tired when she got home, so he would make her dinner. He went back up Avenue A to buy her some books at Mast, then to the grocery store, stopping to smell the cut flowers outside. But the posters they hung in the window, the pictures of pork chops and heads of lettuce and boxes of crackers all with prices written under them, were devastating; bright and gloating. How could they make you pay for something you needed just to survive? He stood on the street in front of the automatic doors and wept.

When he thought about Navas leaving, he couldn't breathe.

I t was dark when I arrived back in Piraeus, and raining. I
sat in a café by the docks drinking Turkish coffee until the
sky grew lighter, then took a train into Athens. I was unrec-
ognizable now. My hair down to my chin. I wore a short skirt
and leggings that I'd taken from the closet, pulled low beneath my belly; wore Milo's T-shirt and sweater and a jacket
I'd found on the boat.

Declan was not at Athens Inn, which meant he was running a train, had another job, or had finally been killed working. I asked at the desk if he'd been around and the
receptionist pretended he didn't exist. So I spent a day walking through Monastiraki and sitting outside the Acropolis,
looking for the right woman to be. Someone small, round.
A pregnant woman. Someone with money, with nice clothes.
Someone wearing makeup; dark hair, short or cut neat. People climbed the stairs in the nearly still mist and disappeared
inside the gateway to the ruin.

Finally I saw her coming down the steps. One of those people who wore special shoes for hiking. She looked strong, American by her style of dress and the bottle of water. She had a camera bag around her neck. A green raincoat with the hood up. I followed her.

The presence of money was clear in the way she moved and I figured she wasn't staying far from there. I kept a few yards behind in the crowd and hoped she wasn't heading to Luzani, where I might be recognized.

But she walked to the Airotel Parthenon, all white and glass, inside draperies and rugs and two chandeliers over the long reception desk, leather furniture in the lobby. She wasn't alarmed by my going up in the elevator with her. People find nothing threatening about a pregnant woman, and only consider the poor distasteful and beyond talking to.

In the silent carpeted corridor I stood next to a cart loaded with towels and soaps while she strolled to her room. After waiting ten minutes I knocked and said the word *housekeeping*, and she opened the door even though I made no attempt to disguise my voice with an accent. She was already wearing a different dress.

I shut and locked the door and then walked past her into the room, and still it took her a minute to understand that I wasn't there to clean it; she was used to people who looked like me doing things for her.

"Can I help you?" she asked.

"Yeah," I said. "I need your clothing and some money and your passport."

She went quickly for the phone but I grabbed it, unplugged it, and threw it across the room. She looked stronger than I was but she was frightened of the unexpected and had learned to do nothing when she was afraid.

"I'm not robbing you," I told her.

"What are you doing, then?" she asked quickly, her breath tight in her chest.

I looked at the shirt lying on the bed, figured she had more dresses in the closet or her suitcase I could wear.

"Are you okay?" she asked, her voice trembling and filled with either compassion or guile. "Do you need to see a doctor?"

"I'm fine," I told her. I sat down on the bed. "Please give me your passport and your purse and I'd like to wear the clothes you were wearing when you walked from the Acropolis."

I reached into my bag and she started to cry a little.

"Okay," I said. "I do need your help."

But I didn't know what to say after that.

I watched her eyes studying my clothing, my face, my belly.

"I'd be happy to give you money for food or whatever you need," she said, wiping her eyes quickly, impatiently. "You don't have to demand it."

"No, thank you."

"What are you doing?" she asked. "What is it you're *doing*?"

She was nice, but she wasn't the kind of person who

would have offered me anything if I wasn't capable of hurting her.

"I'm sorry to have to do this," I told her.

I wasn't. I was happy to do it, to correct at least one small part of an error. And she'd be fine, go home and have a story to tell. I wasn't sorry in the least.

"What are you doing in Athens?" she asked quickly, trying to start a conversation. She flinched when I laughed and I could see she thought I was crazy and then I did feel sorry for her and took out my knife.

"Not much," I told her. "Reading, mostly. I think I may have misinterpreted some myths I read as a kid. I'm trying to understand them better."

"Do you need help?" she asked again. But really she was saying "I need help" and had no one to say it to. I watched her struggling to place me, to know anything about me. "Maybe we can work something out," she said, meaning "Maybe I can get you arrested" or "Maybe I can bribe you to leave and then get you arrested."

I said, "You can give me your passport and clothing and purse and not tell anyone about it for a few hours."

"I can just give you some money or buy you a plane ticket, maybe a ferry ticket. Please," she said, "let me help you."

If I was who she thought I was, this is when I'd have hurt her, not agreed to leave. "I don't need a plane ticket," I said.

"Where are you from?"

"Washington State," I told her, and at this she looked even more startled.

"You're American," she said.

I didn't bother to answer. I could no longer admit to anything as criminally stupid as having a nationality.

"Do you need money?" she asked. "For . . ." She gestured at my body.

"I'm sorry," I said, standing up and holding the knife to her throat. "But I really got to get going." She made a sound in her mouth but no attempt to struggle. When she started crying I wiped the tears from her cheeks with my thumb. And then I really was sad that she was so adept at agreeing to things she didn't want. Her skin felt hot and she was trembling. "It's okay," I told her, trying to calm her, brushing her hair back from her forehead. "It's okay," I said. "After this, you'll be stronger and things won't seem that bad."

The whites of her eyes grew large as she held herself still. She was weak and filled with abeyant terror. And I was happy to separate her from some of the little objects that'd held her down for so long.

The name on her passport was Sutton Rowe. She lived in Bridgeport, Connecticut, was eight years older than me. Her clothes fit fine. I put the skirt and Milo's shirt into my book bag. Looked at myself in the mirror waiting for the elevator. I couldn't pass for her but I could pass for a frightened pregnant tourist who'd just been robbed and who had nice clothes and enough money to be paid attention to.

The rain had let up. I got a cab to Athens Inn and walked

through the lobby as if I were staying there. The linen closet was easy to break into by slipping the knife between the door and the wall. Inside, the air was stale and smelled of him, an acrid undertone of leather and blood. His cot was unmade, a pile of clothes on top. Multiple versions of the same outfit. Levi's and white T-shirts folded and neatly stacked, and a pair of running shoes. He was in Athens. Wouldn't have left the place in this state otherwise; with any luck he was running a train and would be back within an hour or two. There was a large tin of Barry's tea on the side table; an electric kettle, a beaten copy of *The Haw Lantern* lying open and facedown to keep a page. And there was an envelope of photographs: places and people in Athens as well as his usual trophy shots. I went through them to make sure there weren't any of me or Milo. There were two of Jasper; one of him grinning, with a bottle in his hand in the bar of the train, and another of him standing out on the street, smirking, about to say something. I jammed them into my pack before they could do their terrible work on me; I did not need to be reduced to begging a silent empty space for the return of someone I had half imagined.

I took a pair of jeans off the top of the pile and slipped Sutton's passport and two of the three Milo'd given me into the back pocket, laid them out as if he'd just been wearing them. Put Murat's papers on the table with his maps. Then I set Sutton's purse on the floor by his bed, took out her Social Security card, memorized the number, looked at her license, and memorized her address. She was a good three inches taller than me but there was nothing to be done about it.

The district station was in a large municipal building with columns and marble stairs, a Stalinesque construction that had been transformed on the inside into a perfect replica of a dingy booking office in a cop movie: drop ceilings, bright flickering fluorescent lighting. A man in a uniform with a black moustache and light eyes sat at a desk near the door eating an ear of roasted corn on a stick.

"I've been robbed," I said, trying to sound indignant and frightened. "My passport has been stolen! And my purse . . . I saw the man; he ran into a hotel. Athens Inn, it's just down the street! I saw him! He's there now, I'm sure. He threatened me with a knife." I tried to cry but couldn't do it. I gave a detailed description of Declan. "Maybe he's still there now!"

The man listened to me, squinting. He put his hands up, pushed at the air, some kind of sign to make me slow down, got on the phone, and spoke in Greek while I stood there trying to behave like Sutton had when I took her things.

Eventually two uniformed men came out front to stand by the desk and spoke with me in broken English until a gray-haired man in a jacket and tie came over and asked me questions. He had an officious halting accent that sounded like he'd learned English from watching British sitcoms. I told them I was sure the criminal was there now, said I'd be able to identify him, and gave them Sutton's hotel address where they could reach me if they found him.

"What are you doing here in this neighborhood?"

"Why are you asking what *I'm* doing here?" I put my hand on my belly and leaned against the counter and the men exchanged glances. Got me a chair.

I gave them the rest of Sutton's information. Told them I'd be available to make statements, then pretended I had to meet my husband. It didn't matter if Sutton was out there somewhere telling the whole story about me. Soon I'd be gone. And if they went to Athens Inn, if they started looking through his things, I'd be the least of their concerns.

Once I'd done all I could and left the station, I headed to Drinks Time.

The American passport belonged to a flat-faced thirty-year-old man with a receding hairline named Jared Misnick.

I ordered a Turkish coffee and sat at the bar waiting for Boulous to show up. Finally I asked the bartender if he'd seen him. He pointed to a corner where a group of men had been sitting the whole time. I hadn't noticed them, so silent and still before the television. They were leaning back in their chairs looking up at the screen, transfixed by an image of Dustin Hoffman in terrible broken Coke bottle glasses and a filthy-looking Steve McQueen. They were standing on a windy cliffside talking, but it was dubbed into Greek.

I sat down beside the men. "How's it going?" I asked.

One of them shushed me. Boulous looked closely at my

eyes. Recognized me, looked surprised, then went back to watching TV.

Sentimental music played and Steve McQueen tottered forward, hugged Dustin Hoffman, who cried and kissed him on the neck.

"Hey," I said. They all turned sharply around and glared at me, gestured toward the movie.

"Oh, for Christ's sake." I pulled the passport out of my pocket and held it up, then tossed it out in front of them. Boulous pressed my hand down on the table, covering it with his, then actually nodded once more to the screen, where Steve McQueen was hurling himself and a homemade raft off the cliff into the ocean. The music swelled; ragged, bespectacled Dustin Hoffman stared out into the sea, acting. One of the men at the table wiped tears from his eyes.

When the credits began rolling, Boulous turned to me.

"There's something you found?" he asked.

"I found this and thought you might want it," I told him quick and blank.

"Where is your friends?" Boulous asked. And it seemed more of a warning than a question. He handed the passport to an older man with a stubbly pockmarked face and long eyelashes. The man said something I didn't understand and Boulous spoke with him for several minutes.

"I need to get going," I interrupted them, starting to get up. "Do you want it or not?"

The older man looked up, amused, and Boulous grabbed my wrist and held me there.

"Yes or no?" I said.

Their faces shined with indignant surprise. Finally Boulous said, "This is already ours."

"Then I guess you'll give me a finder's fee."

The third man, the one who'd got misty watching Steve McQueen, started to stand but the older man put a hand on his arm and he sat back down.

"Where did you get it?" the older man asked. His English was perfect.

I said nothing. He put four bills on the table.

"From Declan Joyce," I said. "He lives at Athens Inn."

M ilo read about Murat's release not long before Zenaida came back to reclaim her house on the island. It was the last thing he learned about Bridey. Passports from the original sale and the papers of Murat Christensen were found at Athens Inn; a longtime IRA fugitive had been extradited, charged with trafficking.

The picture of Murat after months in jail was something he shouldn't have looked at.

It was easy to imagine different versions of what she'd done. She'd informed, turned herself in, made a deal, been deported back to the States. Or she'd been caught with the documents and it led to everyone being caught. He imagined her having the baby, or the baby being born dead. The baby, if it lived, would be as old as Navas.

These stories in the paper were the last things she communicated to him about their lives together and the kind of man he was.

When Zenaida came back from her semester in England she read what he'd been writing. He'd nowhere to go, no plan. North Africa, he'd told her. He'd live at a port until he found work. Zenaida said no.

Three years wandering drunk, working odd jobs, sleeping out, ruined, running, ended with a placement exam and classes and within a year a book of poems. He returned to the city where he was born; such a reversal of luck, it was like his life in Athens had never happened. Like he had never trembled with the terror of loving someone.

Milo had planned to make dinner, to write her letter, but the afternoon had gotten away from him and now it was dark. The sounds of a garbage truck and men talking and the hollow clunking of plastic containers and trash being crushed came up from the street. Navas startled him coming in. His drink had tipped over onto the floor and it smelled like candy or cough syrup or disinfectant. He picked it up.

"Where's what's-his-name?" Milo asked. She stood in the doorway and the cool from the corridor wafted toward him. He wondered if it was snowing outside.

"His name's Shaunjaye. You gonna get outta bed?"

"I think you should date a boy with a better name. What's he do besides beat up your brother? What's he do?"

"He's got finals for the Golden Gloves coming up."

"What's he *do*?" Milo asked again. "For money."

"He's working at Foot Locker," she said. "He's there now."

"What's that, like some kind of fetish club?"

She sucked her teeth. "No. It's a shoe store. You gonna get up?"

"I've no problem with you and Juan."

"*Shaunjaye,*" she said, then: "Doesn't matter. No one knows what the fuck you're saying with that speech impediment."

"Accent," he said.

She eyed his mattress, looked around the room, and it was then he realized the can he was holding was half-full.

"I don't mind you and Shaun being here," he said, taking a sip.

"Shaunjaye."

"You always say his last name? That's so oddly formal."

She took the can out of his hand and walked into the kitchen. He could hear her pouring what was left of it down the sink.

"Why'd they ever take that stuff off market?" he called to her.

She appeared in the doorway, looking down at him, her arms folded.

"Come here," he said.

Navas sat on the edge of the mattress.

"Come here," he said again. He put his arms out to her and she laid her head on his chest.

"How was school?" he asked. He closed his eyes and placed his palm against her cheek, felt her breathe.

"Fine," she said. "It was fine."

Outside our room we can hear the sea, the slow roll of waves, people calling to one another in the distance.

Her soft black hair curls at the base of her neck. She has small hands, milk breath, the darkest, brightest eyes. The smell of her skin is a drug and her voice carries the sounds of where we've been; strong and strange, the language before language.

A ferry's ride away, people gaze in awe at a reconstructed ruin.

And at night I wake to hear her, laughing in her sleep.

Acknowledgments

Thanks to Jin Auh, Ira Silverberg, and Kimberly Burns. Thanks to Rebecca Friedman, Alexis Gargagliano, and Millicent Bennett.

Thanks to Julianna Haubner and Loretta Denner.

About the Author

Cara Hoffman is the author of the critically acclaimed novels *So Much Pretty* and *Be Safe I Love You*. She has written for the *New York Times*, *Marie Claire*, *Salon*, and National Public Radio. Her work has received numerous awards and accolades, including a Folio Prize nomination and a Sundance Institute Global Filmmaking Award. She has been a visiting writer at Columbia, St. John's, and the University of Oxford. She lives in Manhattan and is currently at work on her fourth novel.